HIS SECRET SUBMISSIVE

OWNED BOOK ONE

KL RAMSEY

His Secret Submissive Copyright © 2019 by K.L. Ramsey.

Cover design Copyright © 2019 by Miblart

Imprint:Independently published

First Print Edition: August 2019

All rights reserved.

No part of this book may be reproduced, scanned, or distributed in any printed or electronic form without permission. Please do not participate in or encourage piracy of copyrighted materials in violation of the author's rights. Thank you for respecting the hard work of this author.

This is a work of fiction. Names, characters, places, and incidents either are the product of the author's imagination or are used fictitiously, and any resemblance to locales, events, business establishments, or actual persons—living or dead—is entirely coincidental.

PROLOGUE

AIDEN

Aiden Bentley stood in the middle of the boardroom feeling as though he had just been blindsided. He must have reread the text from his wife over a dozen times as if he was expecting it to somehow change. It didn't and he was left having to figure out what the fuck he was supposed to do next because he'd never in a million years believe that his Allison would leave him. But according to her very short and not at all sweet text, she was leaving him to be with her new boyfriend who she'd apparently been seeing for months now. She told him she had already moved her stuff out of the house that very morning, after he left for work and she left the kids at her mother's. His favorite part was where she tried to justify the fact that she cheated on him by pointing out how he was always busy with his company and his political run for the vacant Senate seat and she was feeling neglected. Apparently, her new boyfriend gave her the attention she was craving and fulfilled her like no other man ever had. Allison concluded her text by saying she was too young to be saddled down with a husband who loved his company more than he loved her.

He turned his cell off and cursed and when it didn't help him to feel better, Aiden threw it across the room watching it hit the wall and smash into three pieces. Of course his assistant would choose that moment to walk into the conference room.

"You alright, AJ?" she asked. Aiden couldn't help but give her a smile and nod. Rose Eklund was more than his assistant; she was like the mother he never knew. In fact, she was one of the only people to call him by his childhood nickname. Well, her and her son, Corbin. Not too many other people even knew him by that name but Rose did. She was his best friend's mother and when he and Corbin opened their company together ten years earlier, she agreed to work for them until they got up and running and she just stuck around. They began their little start- up in Corbin's basement and he was sure Rose agreed to help just to keep an eye on them. They were just kids back then, fresh out of college and with enough ambition between the two of them to be cocky enough to believe they could make something from nothing. Now they were a multi-billion dollar corporation with offices all over the world and he and Corbin had Rose to thank for most of their success. She kept them organized, focused and most of all—grounded.

"I'm fine, Rose," he lied. She shot him a look that told him she wasn't buying what he was selling. Rose could always tell when he and Corbin were being less than truthful with her. As teenagers, they didn't get away with anything. Looking back now, he had to admit he was thankful he had Rose to keep an eye on him. After his mother left when he was just a baby, it was him and his dad. His father did the best he could with Aiden but he never really got over his wife leaving him. Aiden's dad masked his sadness with alcohol and wallowed in the pit of self-pity that consumed him. Most of his time was spent in bars and when he was able to sober up enough for a job, he worked nights. Rose made sure Aiden had a safe place to hang out over at her house. She made him do his homework and even fed him dinner. Most nights, he'd crash at Corbin's house and Rose would feed him breakfast and make sure he had clean clothes and lunch money. Aiden didn't know where he would have ended up if it hadn't been for her and Corbin basically taking him in.

"Would you like for me to wait here for the truth or do you want to come and find me after you come up with a better story?" Rose crossed her arms over her chest and cocked an eyebrow at him. Aiden didn't hide his amusement especially when she did her best to try to hide her smile.

"You might be part witch," Aiden teased. "How do you always know?"

Rose shrugged, "Mother's instinct, I guess," she said. "So, would you like to try your answer again?"

Aiden wasn't sure if he should tell Rose about Allison's text. Hell, he wasn't sure he understood everything yet and he needed to pick up the girls before Allison's mother got sick of babysitting them and dumped them off at his office. He knew he didn't want the news of his wife leaving him for another guy to work its way around the company and he damn sure didn't need it leaking out into the press. They'd have a field day with the prospective Senator who couldn't keep a leash on his wife. If they only knew the half of it they'd make minced meat out of him and he could kiss his political career goodbye.

"You can't tell anyone this—not even Corbin yet. Promise me, Rose," he said. She looked him up and down as if he lost his mind. Aiden wasn't sure she was going to make him any guarantees to keep her mouth shut and that would mean he had no one to confide in.

"You can't expect me to keep anything from my only son," she chided. Hearing her call Corbin her only child smarted a little. He had to admit he'd like to think she considered him a son too, but he knew that might be asking too much. Rose was right. Asking her to keep a secret from Corbin wasn't fair to either of them.

"Fine, I'll tell Corbin tomorrow. For now, can this remain between the two of us?" he asked. Rose gave a curt nod and he let out the breath he didn't know he was holding. "Allison left me. She just let me know, by text," he admitted.

"By text?" Rose shouted. "How could she do that to you? Oh you poor thing," she sympathized. Rose crossed the room to pull Aiden in for one of her famous mama bear hugs he and Corbin like to tease her about. But instead of leaving him feeling like he wanted to poke fun of Rose, he felt more ready to cry on her shoulder. She held him with no signs of letting him go any time soon and Aiden wrapped his arms around her waist, knowing resistance was futile.

"She can't just take the girls away from you, Aiden. Did she tell you where she went?" Rose asked.

Aiden barked out his laugh, "Yeah, I'm pretty sure she went to live with her boyfriend. Apparently my loving wife has been cheating on me for a half a year now." He pulled free from Rose's hold and she let him go, seeming to know he needed some space.

"I never liked her," she insisted. Aiden shot her a disbelieving look and she shrugged. "Well, it's true, honey. I thought she was just playing you from the start," she admitted. Aiden knew a good many people felt that way, Corbin included. On the day of his wedding, Corbin pulled him aside and begged him not to go through with it. He tried to convince Aiden that Allison was just out for his money, but he was determined to see marrying her through. Allison was five months pregnant with Lucy at the time and he didn't want his kid to grow up without both parents like he had. He saw no other way around marrying Allison and when she agreed to sign the prenuptial agreement, he thought for sure Corbin and everyone else was wrong about her.

For a while, they were happy; especially after Lucy was born. Two years later, they had Laney and he was sure he'd never been happier in his life. He had a gorgeous wife and two beautiful daughters—what more could he ask for? The answer to that was a hell of a lot more complicated than he'd ever care to admit. For as much as he wanted to blame Allison, she was right. He spent late nights at the office and at political functions, trying to fundraise for his run for Senate. Maybe it was all a ruse to cover up the fact he wasn't happy at home, he never really was. He loved Allison and the girls, but he wasn't being completely honest about who he was with his wife or himself. He needed more and that usually left him feeling like a complete ass. Aiden worried there was something wrong with him. Hell, he even went as far as going to see a therapist to help him get over those feelings that plagued him daily.

He was dominant and his need to control and be in charge didn't end when he left the boardroom. He wanted to introduce that side of himself into his marriage, but when he brought up the topic with Allison, she shut him down telling him it wasn't her thing. He tried to tell her they could begin slowly and only incorporate things she would enjoy doing with him in the bedroom but she wasn't willing to even hear him out. His therapist told him he had two choices—either accept his wife's denial and his marriage the way it was or leave. Aiden decided to stay and try to work through his needs and desires, for the sake of his family. His girls deserved more than a father who'd walk away from them so easily. The press shoved the idea of his perfect little family to the masses and voters seemed to eat it up with a spoon. On the outside to everyone looking in, he was a normal business owner with the perfect family life. Aiden was the small town boy who made good and a loyal family man and that was the persona he decided to stick with. That guy got votes. Aiden wasn't sure if he'd be so public friendly when everyone found out what kind of kinks he liked in the bedroom. The only people who truly knew who he was were Allison and Corbin.

"I don't want to get into this now," Aiden admitted. Rose shot him a sympathetic look and he hated knowing that once word got out, everyone would be looking at him the same way. "I have to go pick up Lucy and Laney. Allison left the girls with her mother. She doesn't know if she can be a mom to them right now," he said. He hated how his wife could walk away from their daughters. He knew firsthand what it felt like to know that your own parent didn't want you. He would never let his girls feel unwanted or unloved. At thirty-two he was still living with the demons of being abandoned by his mother after birth and he wouldn't let his daughters be consumed by that same darkness.

"She just left those sweet babies?" Rose choked. Aiden nodded his head, too raw from the emotions roiling through him. He needed to get to his girls and make sure they were both alright. God only knew what Allison had told them and it might be up to him to explain their Mommy wasn't coming home again. He'd just have to find a way to give them the truth without breaking their hearts.

"Okay, you go get the girls and call me later to let me know you are all home safely," Rose ordered. "I'll keep this information to myself but you need to tell Corbin. He loves you like a brother and there isn't anything he wouldn't do for you and the girls." Aiden nodded again and kissed Rose's cheek.

"Thank you," he said. "I'll probably be working from

home for the next few days, just until I can get the girls settled and make some sense out of all of this," he said.

Rose shooed him out of the room, "Go, I've got this. You just go and fix your family," she said. Aiden wanted to tell her it was going to take a damn miracle because he was pretty sure his family was broken beyond repair. He just didn't know how to tell her it was just as much his fault as it was Allison's.

Aiden pulled up to his mother-in-law's home to find Connie waiting on the porch for his arrival, almost as if she was expecting him. He wondered just how long she had been standing out there. "It's about damn time," she shouted at him before he was even completely out of his SUV. "I've been waiting for over an hour for you to show up. Allison told me she texted you and you were on your way here to get the girls and then she disappeared. She didn't even say goodbye to them and now they're upset and asking when she's coming home."

"Did Allison tell you where she was going?" Aiden carefully asked. He hated that he might have to break the news to Connie too, but he was starting to see Allison left him quite a mess to have to clean up.

"Nope," she admitted. "Allison just showed up here out of the blue and told me she needed me to watch the girls. When I said I couldn't because I had a doctor's appointment, she promised you would be right over. I've missed my appointment and now I can't get back in to see him for another two weeks," Connie groused.

"What am I supposed to do for my blood pressure medicine until then?"

"I'll take care of making you another appointment and getting you your medication," Aiden promised, making a mental note to have Rose do that for him in the morning. He hated that Allison would put her mother's health in jeopardy to run off with some guy. Of course, he hated even more he was going to have to be the one to tell her mother that. "I'm afraid I have some bad news," he said. "You might want to sit down for this next part." Connie found her rocking chair in the corner of the small porch and sat down.

"I'm all ears," she said, smiling up at him. "I have a feeling my daughter has gone and done something stupid and I'm looking forward to the part where you defend her bad behavior." Aiden shot Connie an apologetic look, knowing she was probably right. He was always sticking up for his wife when she would make a decision that seemed to hurt everyone around her. Maybe it was the guilt he lived with for wanting more or maybe he was just blind and stupid.

"I don't know that I'll be able to defend her behavior this time, Connie," he admitted. "I got a text from her saying she's left me and the girls." Connie's gasp answered his question for him. He wanted to ask her if her daughter had shared the fact she was so easily abandoning her family or if Allison truly just dumped the girls off and left. "So, you really didn't know, did you?"

"No," she stuttered, raising a shaking hand to her mouth. "How could Allison do that to you and her daughters?" she questioned.

"I have no idea, really. I mean, she mentioned something about having a boyfriend for the past six months and well, maybe I don't blame her. She said I wasn't the best husband and she wasn't all wrong. I spent a lot of late nights at the office and campaigning. Maybe if I had paid more attention to her, this wouldn't have happened," he admitted. He decided to leave out the part about craving a kinkier lifestyle and possibly pushing Allison away when she flat out told him no. Maybe this whole mess was his fault.

"Now there you go," Connie chided. "Allison has admittedly been cheating on you for six months and you blame yourself. God Aiden, you were just providing for your family. My girl was never going to settle down and be happy. Not with you or anyone else, for that matter. Allison was always looking for the next best thing in her life and never stopped to look at what she already had. I'm sorry she did this to you and the girls." Aiden gave a nod not knowing what else to say. She could deny him having anything to do with Allison leaving but he knew the truth. It had been about a year since he came clean and asked Allison to try some of the things he had been wanting. He wasn't asking her to go to a BDSM club from the get-go, but he hoped she'd want to try at least some of the stuff he asked for. It was a lifestyle he knew well, having lived it for most of his twenties. When he met Allison, he was almost twenty-eight and he worried he would never find a woman to settle down with if he didn't leave the BDSM scene and give up his kinky lifestyle. So he did. He started dating Allison and he pushed down that side of himself, never letting on what he needed and everything he craved from her in the bedroom. But Aiden wasn't really happy and he knew if he continued to live a lie, he'd end up hurting them both. He was toying with telling her, but then she announced she was pregnant with Lucy and he got caught up in the excitement of a baby and a wedding. He decided to wait and spring his news on her after Lucy was born and they were officially man and wife. He had some crazy notion that as his wife she'd want the same things he did but he was wrong. In fact, the only thing he had been right about this whole time was the fact his lie would end up tearing them apart. He hated he was correct about that and especially hated how his girls would be the ones to pay the price.

"Listen, I have to get the girls home and tell them about their mother," he all but whispered. He really didn't want to have to do this next part but he had no choice. The three of them were going to have to get used to living without Allison and the sooner he told Lucy and Laney, the sooner they could begin the healing process of moving on. Connie nodded at the front screen door to where both girls stood, watching him. He could tell by Lucy's confused expression she had heard most of their conversation and she had questions.

Aiden opened the door and pulled both girls into his arms. "Hi babies," he murmured. "I'm going to take you home from Nanny's today," he said. Allison was usually the one to pick the girls up from her mother's on the days Connie watched them. Allison called her time away from them her "me time" and insisted it made her a better wife and mother. Now, Aiden could guess her "me time" involved her meeting up with her current boyfriend and he almost wanted to laugh at the irony of it all.

"Where's Mommy?" Lucy questioned. "She usually picks me and Laney up." His four year old was usually very inquisitive and he knew now would be no exception. She would ask him for answers and Aiden worried he wouldn't have any to give.

"Mommy had to go away for a while," he said. "I'm so sorry, girls but Mommy won't be coming home."

"Ever?" Lucy questioned. Laney stood next to her sister, watching between her and Aiden, as if watching a volley. At two, she wasn't a talker like Lucy had been. Laney was more reserved and observant, but he knew she understood everything they were saying. He wouldn't lie to either of them, ever.

Aiden shook his head, "No baby, not ever. You're Mommy had some things to do but I'm here and I won't ever leave you," he promised. Lucy gave him a look that told him she didn't believe him, but that was par for the course. He knew both girls were closer to Allison; she was the parent who was around the most for them. If he was going to earn their trust and help them through this process, he was going to have to make some changes. The first being he needed to be home more often and let Corbin pick up some of the slack around the office. He needed to show the girls he was going to step up and be the parent they deserved, unlike his own dad after his mother left him. He'd never turn into his father. That wasn't even an option—his girls deserved so much better than a drunk who was unreliable at best.

"How about we go home and I'll make us some pancakes for dinner like I used to. Then we can talk this all out and you can ask me all the questions you'd like." Lucy looked him over, as if deciding if she wanted to go with him or stay with Connie. He didn't want to admit he was holding his breath waiting for her agreement but he was. Sometimes negotiating with Lucy was like trying to reason with a tiny terrorist who knew the ins and outs of the system. She knew just what to say and how to work over the person she was up against and Aiden worried she was already smarter than he was.

"Can we have chocolate chips in our pancakes? Lucy asked, looking at Laney to back her up. When the two year old eagerly nodded her head, Aiden couldn't help his chuckle.

"I think I can arrange that," he promised.

"And cream?" Laney chimed in. Aiden was sure his daughters would eat whipped cream on everything if he allowed it.

"Sure, baby girl. We can have whipped cream on top. Any other demands, ladies?" he teased. The girls looked at each other as if silently communicating, trying to decide if they would have any further stipulations to joining him for dinner.

Connie giggled from behind him. "I think your Lucy might just become a hostage negotiator," she teased. "They sure do have your number, Aiden."

"They've always been able to twist me around their little fingers, even Allison," he murmured. He knew it was going to take time to get over his wife. He loved her, but that didn't stop the pain or hurt she caused by walking away. Aiden knew from experience that would take time and might never completely happen for him or his girls.

"So, what's it going to be?" he expectantly asked. Both girls nodded their little blonde heads and smiled up at him.

"We'll take your offer," Lucy agreed as if she had just brokered a business deal. "Thanks, Daddy." She kissed him on his cheek and Laney did the same. He watched as they both ran into Connie's house to get their things.

"Thanks, Connie," he said.

"No need to ever thank me," she offered. "Just call me when you're ready to venture back into the world and I'll help keep the girls as much as I can," she said. Aiden appreciated the offer, but knowing his mother-in-law had health issues would put a damper on him asking too much of her. He loved her for making the offer.

"Will do," he said. Lucy and Laney ran from the front door and over to Connie to kiss her cheek, shouting their goodbyes as they raced to his SUV.

"Come on, Daddy," Laney bossed. He watched as his resilient girls climbed into the back of his vehicle and he wasn't sure how he had gotten so lucky. Aiden wished the promise of chocolate chip pancakes with whipped cream could fix all their problems long term. But for now, he'd take all the help he could get, even if it was only a short term fix.

Aiden got the girls fed and bathed before Corbin showed up to his house. From the sympathetic expression on his face, Corbin had been completely filled in on all of the sordid details. There was only one person who could have clued him in and Aiden wasn't sure if he wanted to thank Rose or ring her neck for sharing his secret. Honestly, he knew Corbin would always have his back and having someone to talk to would be a great help. In just two short hours, Aiden had worked through his self-pity over his wife walking out on him and had already moved straight on to anger. He just hoped he could get the girls to bed before he took his newfound feelings out on them. It wasn't their fault their mother had up and left him and he needed to remember that.

He met Corbin at the front door and held it open for him. "So, I'm guessing your mother filled you in?" he questioned, already knowing the answer before Corbin nodded his head.

He shot Aiden a sheepish grin, "Don't be mad at Mom, AJ," he said. "She's worried about you, man. You know she thinks of you as a son and hell, your girls might be the only grandchildren that woman might ever get. I'm not ready to settle down and have any of the little beasties myself." Corbin grimaced and shuttered from just the thought of having kids and Aiden laughed. His best friend never seemed to understand why he wanted to settle down and have a family. When Aiden and Allison announced she was pregnant,

Corbin's first question was whether or not she was going to keep the baby. Looking back now, that might have been the first clue he had his wife and his best friend weren't going to be each other's biggest fans. Aiden had to run quite a bit of interference back then. After the girls were born, they both seemed to settle down and Aiden could let his guard down a little.

"You're not here to say you told me so, are you?" Aiden grouched. "If you are, you can just turn right around and leave."

Corbin held his hands up in defense, "Naw, man. I'm here to tell you I'm sorry you and the girls have to go through this. I love you like a brother, man. I would never want for any of this to happen no matter what differences I had with Alli," he offered.

Aiden smiled at the nickname only Corbin call his wife. "You know she fucking hated when you called her that, man," Aiden said.

Corbin's wolfish grin said it all. "I know. It's mostly why I did it," he admitted. "How about a beer?" he asked, holding up the six-pack his had hidden under his suit jacket.

"Sure," Aiden agreed. "Make yourself at home. I'm going to tuck the girls in and I'll be right back down," he said. Corbin pulled his tie loose and by the time Aiden got back downstairs, twenty minutes later, his friend had stripped out of his dress shirt and was just wearing one of Aiden's t shirts and a pair of his gym shorts.

"I hope you don't mind me borrowing some clothes," Corbin said.

Aiden laughed. "No problem. Although I'm afraid

you're going to stretch out my shirt," he teased. Corbin worked out daily and he was bigger than Aiden, always had been. His arms alone looked like two of Aiden's put together. The women in town seemed to appreciate Corbin's gym efforts and loved the tattoos that banded his arms. Corbin usually kept them hidden under his dress shirt and jacket but when they would all casually go out for drinks, he basically had to turn women away left and right. Women fell for his good guy persona wrapped up in his bad boy image. Aiden had never seen the appeal of tattoos, even if the women seemed to go a little crazy over them. He had one tattoo on his upper arm of a shark wearing swim trunks and sunglasses. Aiden usually kept it secretly tucked away under his suits during the day, but it was his harsh reminder of drunken bad decision made with Corbin while they were pledging the same fraternity in college.

"I ordered pizza too. I haven't had time to eat all day and I'm starving," he said. As if on cue, the pizza delivery guy showed up with Corbin's extra-large meat lovers' pizza that made Aiden's mouth water. He paid the delivery guy and they both settled in the family room with their beer and pizza. Aiden could feel Corbin was holding back with him, like he was keeping his hand close to his vest.

"All right, man let's have it. I know you're dying to say your peace, so spill it," Aiden insisted.

"I really don't have anything to say you haven't heard before, man. I hate to say, 'I told you so'," he lied.

"You'd fucking love to tell me you were right. In fact, I'm betting you love saying those words to me more than you love pussy and that's a whole fucking lot," Aiden teased. Corbin stroked his beard and looked over at Aiden as if he was trying to decide if he was right or not.

"Well, you're not completely wrong but I guess it just depends on the pussy," Corbin joked. Corbin and he might have been the same age but his best friend was always taking lead when it came to their relationship. He seemed to think Aiden needed protecting, being smaller than him growing up and who knows, maybe he was right. It sure felt good to have Corbin in his corner no matter what he was up against. It was one of the reasons Aiden chose to go to the same college as him, not ready to part ways with the person who stuck by him through thick and thin. Corbin was basically his brother and he wasn't sure what he would do without him.

"So what now?" Aiden asked. "Allison left me with two little girls who are probably going to grow up without a mother. How do I fix that?" Aiden took a swig of his beer and tossed his half eaten pizza back into the box.

"You don't fix it, man. You be the best dad you can be and show your girls when life gives you shit, you find your shovel," Corbin growled. "How do you know Alli won't be back, AJ?" he asked. Yeah, he hadn't gotten to the best part of his day yet—the part where Lucy handed him her backpack and told him Mommy left something inside for him. Allison apparently told the girls to wait to give him the letter she wrote until they were home from Connie's house. He had to hand it to his wife, she sure knew how to bring the drama. At least he could read her letter in the privacy of his own home and this time, when he finished reading it, he could just tear it up and throw it away. His poor phone bore the extent of his anger at her earlier text and now he was going to have to run out and pick up a new one in the morning.

"Allison left me a letter with the girls. She told them to give it to me when we got home from Connie's," Aiden admitted.

Corbin whistled, "Wow, she had this all planned out, didn't she? What did it say?" he asked.

"Basically, she said she wasn't cut out to be a wife or mother and she wasn't willing to spend her life wondering, 'What if?'. She told me to text her when the divorce papers were ready to be signed and she didn't want anything but the money that was promised to her when she signed the prenup."

"And how much is that?" Corbin angrily barked.

"One and a half million." Aiden shrugged.

"Fuck, man," Corbin swore. Aiden didn't hide his smile. Corbin seemed angrier than he did about the day's events, if that was even possible. Honestly, Aiden just felt numb about the whole thing now. He wasn't sure that was going to change any time soon either.

"It's only money, man," he said. He meant it too. He'd pay just about any amount to have Allison be a part of the girls' lives but he knew once his wife made up her mind, there was no changing it. She chose to walk away from him and his daughters and now, the three of them would be the ones paying the price.

"How about you take some time—you know figure out just what you and the girls need. I'll handle the majority of the work stuff and that way you have time to focus on your family and politics," Corbin offered.

"I can't just dump the company on your lap, man," Aiden said. "I'll handle my own shit but I'm going to take the next two weeks off. I need to figure out the girls' schedules and make sure they are both alright with everything that is changing. Maybe we'll take a quick trip somewhere, get out of town for a few days—you know the whole change of scenery thing?" Aiden didn't really have a plan but as far as ideas went, a little family trip sounded like a good one.

"That sounds like a good plan," Corbin confirmed. "Get the girls minds off of missing Alli and you can take some down time."

"Right. I'll have Rose book us something in the morning," Aiden agreed. Corbin shot him a concerned look and Aiden chuckled. "Don't worry, man, I'll be fine. Allison made her decision and we will just have to live with it. Life marches on, as your mom likes to say."

"Yeah," Corbin agreed. "I always hated that expression I just never had the balls to tell her," he admitted. Aiden threw back his head and laughed and for the first time since getting Allison's text, he felt normal, as if everything was going to be alright. He just wished he believed it because Aiden wasn't sure anything would be right ever again.

ZARA

6 months later

Zara Joy walked into the local club and she wasn't sure how she let her best friend talk her into this. A night club was one thing but the town's only BDSM club was quite another. She was sure she wasn't going to be able to follow through with the dare she accepted and would run out of there like the meek little mouse she was. When Avalon tricked her into agreeing to step out of her comfort zone, she had no clue it would be this far out. Her comfort zone was a distant blip on her radar and Zara wasn't sure if she'd ever be able to find her way back again. But once Ava found out she hadn't lost her virginity, as she falsely reported the one and only time the subject came up, she went off and dared her to do the unthinkable.

Truthfully, she wanted a change from her everyday pace and when Ava told her about a new club in town, she was intrigued. The idea of dancing the night away left Zara feeling daring and ready to take on Ava's challenge. But her sneaky friend never mentioned the new club wasn't a night club but a sex club that catered to the elite clientele who paid hefty fees to join. Ava's father owned half the town so she had no problem getting Zara into the club as a guest for the night.

Zara's cell rang and she pulled it from her purse. "Hello," she whispered.

"Hey girl," Ava sassed, "Did you make it to the club alright?" she asked. Ava knew damn well Zara wouldn't be able to resist a dare. Zara held the phone away from her face and put her on speaker so Ava could hear the moans and groans of pleasure filling the club. A woman was in the corner, sprawled across and bound to what looked like a saddle, having her ass spanked red by a man standing behind her with a leather paddle. She hoped Ava would be able to hear the sound of the paddle every time it made contact with the woman's fleshy ass or the way she cried out and then moaned with pleasure.

"Does it sound like I'm at the club?" Zara asked.

Ava giggled into the other end of the cell. "I knew you wouldn't turn down a good dare."

"Yeah well, I thought you were sending me to an actual club, not a meat market of naked women getting men off," she whispered. "What the actual hell, Ava?"

Her giggle filled the other end of the line again and she knew their conversation was going nowhere. "You should totally take advantage of one of those men, Z," Ava said. "You're a twenty-five year old virgin and it's time for you to drop that title." Ava was right but what was she supposed to do? Walking right up to some leather clad man welding a whip didn't seem like the best idea. Zara was sure that scenario playing out wouldn't end well for her.

"I can't just walk up to a complete stranger and ask him for sex," Zara spat.

"Oh, I don't know. You might find some of us complete strangers are open to a little fun, honey. That is why most of us are here." Zara spun around and found a man standing so close to her, she could feel his breath on her skin. He was sexy as sin, impeccably dressed in a three piece suit with his light brown hair disheveled as if someone had run their fingers through it already. His blue eyes were what caught her off guard. They were so dark that him looking at her felt as if he could see directly into her soul, even eliciting a shiver from her.

"I'm sorry," she said, taking a step back from him. "I was having a private conversation with my friend." She held up the phone as if proving a point. "Ava," she said into the phone, realizing her so called friend had hung up on her. "Fuck," she cursed. The sexy man's smirk was nearly her undoing and she found herself smiling back at him for no real reason.

"Seems your friend had other plans then to talk on the phone all night. You have any other plans Miss—" He looked her up and down as if waiting her out. Zara thought not answering him might be her best bet but the way he looked at her, as if he wasn't giving her an option but to answer, she had no choice.

"Zara," she answered. He gifted her with his sexy

smirk again and she was sure her panties were going to burst into flames from just the scorching way he looked her up and down. It was almost territorial, like he was marking her with his gaze.

"Nice to meet you, Zara. I'm Aiden," he said holding his hand out to take hers. She hesitantly took his offered hand and gave a gentle shake, noting the way he didn't take his eyes from hers. "Is this your first time here?" he asked. Zara nodded and pulled her hand back from him.

"I'm here because of a stupid dare," she admitted. God, she sounded like a child and she wished she could take back her words. "Um, I mean my best friend dared me to go out to a club by myself and well, I thought she meant a regular club—you know like dancing and drinks." Aiden smiled at her and she felt like a giddy schoolgirl. "Instead, she sent me here and well, this wasn't what I had imagined," she admitted.

"You don't sound very happy about being here, Zara. Would you like to leave?" That was a very good question. She looked around the room as if trying to decide her answer. A part of her was curious and she had to admit the chances of her returning were slim to none. What would it hurt to take a look around and maybe get a little bit of experience? No one knew who she was or that she was a virgin, at least she hoped they didn't. Last time she looked, it wasn't stamped on her forehead or anything.

"I think I'd like to stay," she almost whispered. Zara didn't turn to look at him, fixated on the woman in the corner of the room she saw earlier. The man who had been spanking her while she was strapped to a leather saddle released her bonds and was fucking her from behind, in front of the whole room. People had stopped what they were doing to watch the two of them together and Zara felt like an intruder. She wanted to look away but she couldn't. They were seriously hot together and the way he commanded her body made Zara feel things she never had before.

"You like watching them?" Aiden whispered into her ear. She nodded and smiled back over her shoulder to where he stood. He was so close again she wondered if this guy had any personal space boundaries.

"I—I think I do," she shyly admitted. If she was being completely truthful, she would have told him she wasn't sure what she liked and didn't like because she was never with a man before, not in that way. Sure, she had dated her fair share of guys over the years, but working as a nanny didn't afford her the luxury of meeting too many people on the job. It wasn't like she could have an office romance or go out for drinks with her co-workers after the day was over. She usually lived with the families she nannied for making it hard for her to have any sort of social life. Zara never really had friends over to the family's house, not wanting to presume that was alright. Besides Ava, she really didn't have many other friends but she wasn't lonely. She loved her work and the families whom she grew to think of as hers especially since she didn't have one of her own.

"Would you like to try the spanking bench?" Aiden asked.

"Um, shouldn't we get to know each other first or something?" she questioned. Zara felt silly asking but this whole thing felt completely foreign to her. When she thought about having sex for the first time, she imagined the guy would at least buy her dinner first. Never in her wildest dreams did she think he'd be asking to spank her ass red while she straddled a leather saddle.

Aiden's chuckle and his warm breath on her shoulder made her shiver. "It was just a question, Zara. Maybe I should have dared you," he teased, causing her to giggle.

"Accepting dares apparently never ends well for me," she murmured.

"Well, maybe tonight will be different," he suggested. "I can help you with that," he offered. Zara wasn't sure how this was all supposed to work but she felt foolish asking.

"I'm not sure I'm ready for all of this—" she said, waving her hands wildly about. "It's just so public," she admitted. Zara felt like a complete fraud standing in the middle of a sexual playroom with no experience of her own.

"Would you like to get a private room?" he asked. She could tell he was trying for nonchalant, but the way he looked at her so intensely, she knew he was hoping she'd say yes. How could she not? He hadn't even really touched her yet and she was sure her panties were wet. She wanted Aiden, that was not the question. Why she wanted a complete stranger might be something she should think about but not now. Right now, she wanted to go with Aiden and take him up on his offer. Zara was done being a coward and it was time she did something about it. She was going to do this for herself. She didn't give a fuck about Ava's dare and when she walked out of that club tonight, she wouldn't' have to look back or wonder about what if's because that wasn't what Aiden was offering her. She might be naïve, but she knew enough to know her handsome stranger was going to give her just what she wanted—a night of strings free hot sex and that was just fine with her.

"Yes," she whispered. "I'd like that, Aiden."

AIDEN

Aiden wasn't sure what had drawn him to the pretty little blonde woman with curves for miles and the sexiest smile he had seen in a long time. Maybe it was the way she seemed so nervous and out of place but he couldn't stay away from her and why should he?

Since Allison left, he had been the picture perfect father. He had taken the girls to the beach for a few days and when they were sick and tired of the sun and sand, he flew them all to Disney and by the time they finally got back home, he felt like he needed a vacation from his vacation. Aiden had worked it out with Connie for her to babysit the girls a few afternoons a week after their preschool let out. He arranged for a car and driver to pick them up from school and deliver them to Connie's to help cut down on her workload. Honestly, it was the very least he could do since she was helping him out so much. Aiden knew it had to be hard on her but she insisted she loved having the girls around. He knew it was good for Lucy and Laney too. Even though they didn't really talk about Allison much, he could tell they both missed her and being with their grandmother seemed to help lift some of their sadness.

Aiden threw himself back into his work and every night after he'd put the girls to bed, he'd fall into his own bed, dog tired. He was ready for a change and a little fun. His divorce was finalized two weeks prior and Allison made no attempts to call or see him or the girls. He had his lawyer send her the divorce papers and the check and that was the only contact they had, which was fine by him. Corbin convinced him to stop working so damn hard and blow off some steam. He told Corbin he was fine but they both knew he was lying. Corbin convinced him to get a sitter and join his local BDSM club. Aiden had to admit he thought his friend was crazy for making the suggestion, but the few times he had been there made him feel alive. And now, the sexy little blonde had agreed to get a private room with him and he was hoping she'd want to play. He could think of nothing he wanted more than to play with sexy little Zara.

Aiden wasted no time showing Zara back to his private room. He kept one reserved knowing anything he did with a woman in the playroom would be in the public eye. When members paid to join the very exclusive club, they were all made to sign a waiver saying what happened in the club would remain private but he knew better. Aiden still had just over six months until the election and there was no way he'd trust everything he'd already built to a simple waiver. People made promises all the time, but enough incentive could persuade anyone to change their minds. He knew he couldn't let anything get in the way of his run for the Senate, not even his driving desires for Dominance. Taking women back to his fully stocked private room seemed to be the only way to ensure privacy. Sure, that meant putting his trust into virtual strangers to keep his secret but what other choice did he have? Meeting women who were into the same kinks he liked wasn't something one could do at a bar or even a dating sight. He couldn't risk the exposure and everything he had worked so hard to build.

He shut the door, closing out the sounds of sultry music, moans and leather slapping bare skin that seemed to play through the club. He was used to the scene by now after a couple of weeks attendance but he could tell this world was new to her. Aiden worried Zara might not be ready for everything he wanted to do with her and he had to know she was completely with him; otherwise he wouldn't move forward with her.

"Is this your first time?" he questioned. The look on Zara's beautiful face was almost comical. She shyly nodded her head and he couldn't help his smirk. Aiden wasn't sure if introducing her to kink was a good idea, but the thought of being the first man to give her a taste of the lifestyle he was quickly coming to love, turned him completely on.

"How about you tell me what you'd like to try and I'll do my best to give it to you?" he asked. It wasn't usually how things worked, but he wanted Zara's first experience with kink to be one that brought her pleasure. Him demanding what he wanted from her might turn her off to the whole world and wouldn't that be a shame?

"I think I'd like to try spanking," she said with a shrug. Aiden smiled; his hand literally felt like it tingled at the thought of smacking her sexy, curvy ass.

"I think I'd like to spank you, Zara," he admitted. He wasn't sure what it was about the woman standing in front of him but his whole body seemed to hum to life just being in the same small room with her. Zara looked shyly at the bed and he could see she was still unsure of everything. He closed the short space between them and wrapped her in his arms, pulling her body snugly against his own. Zara gasped and looked up at him, just the reaction he was hoping for.

"If you don't want to do this, honey we don't have to. We can do as much or as little as you'd like. You're in charge here," he admitted. And he meant it too. She was completely in control of everything they would or wouldn't do tonight—he wouldn't push her into anything she wasn't ready for.

Zara giggled, "I thought you were in charge," she teased. Aiden smiled and dipped to gently kiss her lips and those damn sparks felt as if they ran through his entire body. She shyly kissed him back and he wanted to take more from her but he needed to remember his promise. He was going to let her take lead and tell him what she wanted. Then, he'd find a way to hold his inner caveman at bay long enough to give her what she needed and hopefully she'd ask him for more.

"Wow," she whispered, breaking their kiss. He liked the way he seemed to leave her a little breathless.

"Yeah—wow," he agreed. "Tell me you feel it too," he commanded.

Zara nodded her head, not taking her eyes from his. "Sparks," she said. "I feel them," she admitted.

"Thank fuck," he breathed. "Tell me what else you want me to do to you, Zara," he ordered. His body was ready for more and his dick was twitching to be set free but he needed to be patient. Every urge in his body was telling him to forget all the kink and foreplay, throw sexy little Zara onto his bed and thrust balls deep into her. He wanted to mark her, make her his and never let her out of that fucking room again—but that wasn't what any of this was. He needed to remember she was a stranger in a BDSM club looking for one thing. Sure, it was the same thing he was searching for, but for some reason he seemed to want to take more from the beautiful stranger.

Aiden couldn't seem to help himself; he ran his hands over her curves, kissing his way down her neck. He wanted more from her. Hell, he wanted everything from her. "Well," she stuttered. He loved the way she shivered against his body, seeming to like the attention he was paying her sensitive neck. He ran his hand up under her tank top to find she wasn't wearing a bra and nearly came in his fucking pants. Aiden tugged at her taut nipple, eliciting a gasp and soft moan from Zara.

"You like that?" he asked, already knowing the answer.

"Yes," she hissed.

"What else do you want, Zara?" he once again demanded.

"I want it all, Aiden, please," she begged. He didn't stop this time, pulling her over to the bed with him. He sat on the edge and ran his hands up under her short skirt, cupping her bare ass. He let his fingers flex into her fleshy globes and pushed his face into her pussy. Even through her clothing, he could smell her arousal and he knew she was ready for him.

"Strip," he commanded. Zara hesitated as if she wasn't sure if she wanted to follow his orders or protest. He took his hands off her body as if letting her know she could refuse him but if she did, he wouldn't touch her again. "You don't have to do anything you don't want to, Zara," he admitted. "I won't touch you again until you tell me it's what you want."

Zara reached for his hands and pulled them back to her body. "I want," she admitted. She tugged her skirt down her body to reveal she wasn't wearing any panties either. He hissed out his breath, greedy to taste her. She was gorgeous; her pussy was completely bare, just the way he liked and he could tell she was soaked and ready for whatever he wanted from her. Zara then shyly pulled her tank up over her body, revealing her perfect breasts to him and this time, he didn't stop himself. He pulled her against his body and sucked one of her nipples into his mouth, loving the way she cried out his name. If he had his way, he'd have her panting and needy within minutes.

"You're beautiful, Zara," he whispered into her ear. She gifted him with her shy smile and rubbed her body against his.

"Will you take off your clothes too?" she asked.

Aiden knew if he did, this whole scene would be over way too quickly. It was best if he kept his pants on while she was sprawled across his lap for her spanking. He wanted to at least give her part of her request so he yanked off his dress shirt, loving the way her blue eyes greedily roamed his torso. "You work out way more than I do," she teased. Aiden chuckled against her skin as his lips made their way up to her mouth.

"Working out is a good stress reliever," he admitted. Honestly, sex was an even better stress reliever for him but he didn't get to play like this as often as he'd like. Aiden had only recently joined the club and the first couple times he went, he found himself watching and learning rather than participating. He was perfectly happy to sit back in the shadows and observe but tonight, when Zara walked in, he couldn't help himself. He knew if he didn't jump on her another Dom would and he didn't want to miss his chance with the sexy blonde. Every man in the club seemed to take notice of her, watching to see if she was with anyone. He knew other men would have given just about anything to take Zara back to their room and he counted himself lucky she agreed to accompany him to his private quarters.

"I'm afraid I don't get much time to work out. I lack the free time to just run to the gym," Zara said. She tried to cover herself with her arms and Aiden growled his displeasure. He wouldn't let her hide from him.

"It's too late for that, Zara," he insisted, tugging her arms down from her body. "I've already seen just about every square inch of your body, baby. You are so fucking sexy and I won't have you hiding from me, understand?" he asked. Zara kept her arms at her side, as if accepting his dare and he chuckled. "You really seem to like a good dare, don't you, honey?" he teased.

"Yes," she breathed.

"Good. Let's see how you handle this next one. I dare you to lay across my lap so I can spank that curvy ass of yours," he said. Zara's eyes flared at the mention of him spanking her and he knew he was on the right track with what she wanted from tonight. Aiden sat on the edge of the bed and waited for her to make her decision. He didn't know he was holding his breath until she took a step towards him and he let out his pent- up sigh.

"Like this?" she questioned, laying across his lap with her fleshy ass prominently displayed.

"Yes," he hissed, "just like that, baby." God, this woman might just be his undoing with the way she seemed to obey his every command. She was a perfect submissive and dare he think it—just the type of woman Aiden had been looking for his whole life. He needed to keep his eye on the prize and stop jumping ahead of himself though. Zara was just looking for a hook-up, not a marriage proposal and it would do him well to remember that.

Zara squirmed around his lap and his cock protested that he still had his pants on. When she finally settled, he ran the palm of his hand over her ass, loving the breathy little moans and sighs that escaped her lips. "Ready, baby?" he questioned. Aiden needed to be sure Zara was one hundred percent on board.

"I'm ready," she agreed and settled across his lap. He almost wanted to chuckle when she dramatically exhaled but he didn't dare. He knew that this being Zara's first time experiencing any part of the kinky lifestyle might be a little unnerving for her.

"I'll go slowly and you tell me if you don't like something and we can stop," he offered. "You are in complete control here, Zara," he admitted. She turned her head and smiled up at him. "I'd like for you to keep count," he said. She looked back down to the floor and nodded her agreement. Honestly, he was beginning to feel a little nervous from her jitters and it had been some time since any woman made him feel that way.

He landed the first blow on her left globe and then rubbed his palm over where he left his mark. "One," she choked out. Aiden worried this was all going to be too much for her but he also gave her an out. All Zara had to do was tell him to stop and he would. He landed the second blow on her right cheek, liking to mix things up and not concentrate too much on one area. Although the thought of Zara remembering him every time she sat down tomorrow did strange things to him.

"Two," she said and rubbed her wet folds on his lap. He could feel her heat through his pants and he liked the way she responded to her spankings.

"Hold still, baby," he commanded and brought down his palm again, meeting her fleshy ass.

"Three," she moaned. Aiden couldn't help himself, he needed to know she was enjoying her spanking half as much as he was. He dipped two fingers down into her folds and found her so wet and ready for him that all he could think about was how good she was going to feel when he finally got to the portion of the night where he could take her body. He wanted to be inside of her, claiming her and making Zara cry out his name over and over—but that would come soon enough. First, he needed to finish her spanking and then he'd sink balls deep into her luscious body and take what he wanted from her.

ZARA

Aiden was giving her so much pleasure she wasn't sure if she would be able to take much more. She had just counted out the eighth time his hand landed on her ass and all she could think about was Aiden and what he was going to do to her. Every time his palm made contact with her skin she could feel every promise he was silently making her. Honestly, she knew she should be nervous about what was about to happen between the two of them but she wasn't. Aiden was in control of her body, mind and soul and that seemed to be just what she needed. Zara was able to finally get out of her own head, not think so much about the next step and just feel.

The final blow was a little harder than the rest and she yelped in surprise. It really didn't hurt, just caught her off guard. "Ten," he growled and turned her in his lap. He pulled her up his body, so she was straddling his cock, almost cradling it with her slick folds and she forgot all about not knowing what to do next. The way

Aiden was kissing her was nearly her undoing. No man had ever kissed or touched her the way Aiden was. She couldn't seem to get enough of the way he almost wanted to consume her.

"On the bed, Zara," he said. He helped her free from his lap and she laid back onto the big bed as he ordered. She had to admit she liked his bossy nature; it turned her on. "I'm going to cuff your ankles and wrists to the bed, baby," he said. "Are you okay with that?" Aiden hovered over her body and she wasn't sure how she felt about being bound to his bed. A part of her was afraid that letting a complete stranger shackle her to his bed wasn't such a great idea. For all she knew he could be a crazed lunatic. But when he looked at her, so trusting and hopeful, she wanted to give him everything he was asking for and more.

"Yes," she said, nodding her agreement. "I think I'd like that," she admitted.

"Good girl," he praised. She liked when he called her that. It made her want to please him by continuing to be his good girl. Zara just needed to remember this had nothing to do with emotions or her heart. He wasn't asking her for a commitment. Aiden wanted to use her body for a night of pleasure and that was it. Feelings had nothing to do with what he wanted from her.

Aiden made quick work of securing her ankles and wrists to the bed posts using soft- cuffed hand cuffs. She had to admit being completely bound and spread wide for him both excited her and scared the hell out of her. The way Aiden looked at her made her completely hot. He ran a finger along her cheek and down her neck, making his way to her sensitive nipple. He was working his way down her body and just his simple touch, with one single finger, nearly made her crazy with lust. She bucked and writhed against her restraints and he chided her for not holding still for him.

"Do you want me to stop, Zara?" he sternly questioned.

"No," she stuttered. "Please don't stop," she begged.

"Do you think you can hold still for me while I eat your pussy?" he asked. She wanted to move, to squirm but God she wanted to feel his mouth on her wet core. She wanted to know what it felt like to have a man between her legs in every way and Aiden was promising her that and so much more. All she had to do was hold still. Surely she could do that, right?

"Yes," she hissed.

"Good girl," he praised. Aiden ran two fingers through her drenched folds and moaned. "You are so wet for me, baby," he said. "You are going to feel so fucking amazing when I finally fuck you. I wonder if you taste as good as you feel," he teased. Aiden settled between her thighs and seemed to hesitate. She looked down her body to find him studying her and if she wasn't mistaken, he actually sniffed her pussy.

"You smell so fucking good, honey," he growled. He licked into her folds to find her sensitive clit and sucked it into his mouth. She couldn't help herself, Zara bucked against his mouth, as if trying to take more of what he was already giving her.

"Zara," he warned. She tried to hold still, really she did but just his warm breath on her sensitive core had her writhing and moaning with pleasure. She was so close; she just needed a little more.

"Please," she begged. "Please I need more, Aiden. I'm so close," she cried. She wasn't sure if she was begging him to give her everything or stop. It was almost too much and Zara wasn't sure if she'd ever get enough of the sexy man who was taking complete control of her body.

"I've got you, baby," he promised. "Just lay back and enjoy this and let me take care of you." Zara took a breath and dramatically released it, causing Aiden to chuckle. "Good girl," he praised. Zara wasn't sure why every time Aiden said those words to her, her entire world felt right. Maybe it was the fact he was praising her but really, why should that matter? Aiden was virtually a stranger to her and his opinion shouldn't count—but it did.

Aiden ran his fingers through her wet folds and Zara did everything she could to remain completely still. A soft whimper escaped her lips as she looked down her body to watch Aiden. He smiled up at her and winked and Zara knew he was intentionally driving her crazy. "You're doing this on purpose," she accused.

"Doing what?" he murmured, seemingly distracted by her body.

"Teasing me," she said.

"No, honey," he admitted. "I'm not teasing you. I'm teaching you to hold still for me. You're doing a beautiful job too," he praised. This time she felt less anxious to please him. Truthfully, Zara was feeling a little pissed he might be punishing her in any way.

"That's not fair," she pouted. Aiden laughed against the delicate skin of her inner thighs, working his way back to her aching pussy. He knew exactly what he was doing and it was driving her crazy.

"Fair has nothing to do with it, honey. While you're in this room you belong to me. I do what I please with what is mine and at this very moment in time, you're mine," he said. She wasn't sure how she felt about belonging to anyone but he was right about one thing. At that very moment, she was his and there was nothing she could do about it. Hell, there was nothing she wanted to do about it. She liked the way Aiden controlled her body as if he could read her every need. There was no way she'd want to tell him to stop—not now and probably not ever.

Zara laid back and Aiden seemed to take it as a sign of her compliance. He parted her folds and kissed and sucked at her until she couldn't stand it anymore. "Come for me, Zara," he ordered. She wasn't sure how or why, but her body seemed to do as he asked and she felt as though she was falling and no one would be there to catch her. Zara felt as Aiden tugged her wrists and ankles free from the restraints and gathered her into his arms, pulling her snugly against his body.

"I've got you, baby," he crooned over and over again and for the first time in a very long time, Zara didn't feel so alone. She wrapped her arms around his neck and looked up at him, wanting to say something—anything but she wasn't sure what would be appropriate in this situation. She had never been in this particular circumstance, so she didn't quite know what to do.

"Thank you," she breathed and nuzzled his neck.

"You never have to thank me for giving you an orgasm, honey," he whispered. "We aren't finished here Zara, not by a long shot. I'd like to see you again, after tonight." Once again, she was struck mute. She hadn't gone out expecting to meet anyone. Honestly, she hadn't gone out expecting to end up in a sex club. Meeting someone as wonderful as Aiden threw her for a loop but she wanted to tell him yes. Zara wanted to see Aiden again and she wasn't about to deny him.

"Yes," she murmured. "I'd like to see you again, Aiden," she admitted. He gifted her with his sexy half smirk and she knew any resistance she might have been feeling was now completely gone.

"I want you, Zara," he said. No man had ever said those words to her and she could feel her body hum to life again. He rolled her underneath his body and she had to admit, all the feelings of nervousness and worry seemed to dissipate. She didn't know what it was about this man that made her want to trust him but she did. Maybe that made her a fool but she didn't really care.

Aiden kissed down the column of her neck and back up to her lips, giving her soft, slow, passionate kisses that felt like he reignited a fire deep down in her core. "Please," she whimpered and that seemed to be all he needed. He rolled her underneath his body and plunged balls deep into her core. Zara cried out in pain and Aiden stilled.

"What the fuck, Zara?" he growled. She closed her eyes, not really sure if she was trying to hide from his piercing gaze over the fact she kept she was a virgin from him or from the pain of having him sink into her body.

"I'm fine," she lied.

"You want to tell me what the hell is going on here?" he asked. His question felt more like an accusation.

"Well, I thought we were having sex," she sassed. From the look on his face, he wasn't in the mood for her cheeky remarks. Two could play at that game because she wasn't in the mood to be treated like a child.

"I mean the fact you are obviously a virgin, Zara," he barked.

"I was a virgin, Aiden. You just took care of that issue for me." Again he shot her a disapproving look that should have made her cringe but there was no way she was going to back down—not now. She was a grown woman and she was capable of making her own choices.

"It's no big deal, really," she added. I'm twenty-five and up until a few seconds ago, I was a virgin. It was about time I took care of that little problem," she admitted.

"It wasn't a little problem; it was your virginity. You should have told me or at least given me a heads up. It's almost as if you lied by omission," he accused.

"Are you calling me a liar, Aiden? I might be a lot of things but a liar isn't one of them. I wanted you and you seemed to be pretty into me. I don't understand what the big deal is," she said.

"The big deal is that it was a big fucking deal but you didn't share it with me. As the other person involved here, I had the right to know. Communication is key and you blew that, Zara. You kept a vital piece of information about yourself from me," he said. His tone was harsh and she knew they weren't getting anywhere with their discussion, just moving in circles. She pushed at his body, wanting him out of her. They were still joined and this was definitely not the way she pictured her first time. Hell, none of this was, but Aiden was making fantasies she didn't know existed come true. Maybe this whole night was just a giant mistake but Zara hoped Aiden saying he wanted to see her again was a good sign. Instead, he looked at her like he hated her and all she could think about was getting as far away from him as possible. Aiden took the hint and rolled off her body, allowing Zara to get up. She quickly pulled on her skirt and tank top and found her shoes in the corner of the room. She put them on and grabbed her purse, not wanting to look back at the bed where Aiden was. She couldn't stand the sadness and disappointment that was going to be waiting for her in his eyes. She had already seen enough and all Zara wanted to do was go home and take a long shower, crawl into her own bed and cry herself to sleep. Tomorrow, she could figure out the rest of her crazy mixed-up life.

AIDEN

Aiden spent the next two weeks trying to forget the sexy curvy blonde who haunted his dreams. Every night, as he was about to drift off, he would see Zara slipping on her shoes and not bothering to give him even a second look back. It hurt seeing her walk away but he knew it was for the best. He just needed to figure out why the hell it hurt so fucking much to watch her go. Zara was the first woman Aiden had felt a connection with since Allison left him. It was silly really. He didn't know Zara and feeling butt hurt over a woman he barely spent an hour with was complete nonsense—but that was where he was at. He had a big fundraiser last night and every blonde woman who came into the room reminded him of her. Aiden found himself wishing Zara would magically appear and when she hadn't, he thought about going back to the club and finding another blonde sub to take her place but he knew that wouldn't work either. He had a feeling no one else would measure up to her and he'd end up disappointed and confused.

"Hey man, you look like complete shit," Corbin assessed. He walked into Aiden's office, bypassing his mother's shouts telling him Aiden wasn't to be disturbed.

"It's alright, Rose," Aiden offered. "Corbin doesn't listen to either of us so you might as well save your breath." Corbin smiled and agreed with him, watching Rose shake her head at the pair of them and leave his office. "You know, one of these days she's going to lose her shit with you and just up and quit," Aiden accused.

"Yeah," Corbin said with a shrug. "But today's not that day," he teased. "What's up with you, man? You seem grumpier than usual lately, if that's even possible." Aiden knew Corbin was referring to his shitty moods since his night with Zara in the club but he wouldn't come right out and say it. Aiden had told him all about his sexy little bombshell and the way she used him to lose her virginity. Corbin thought the whole thing was a lot funnier than Aiden did but that was usually the way things worked between the two of them. Corbin was easier going and carefree while Aiden had adult responsibilities—namely two little girls who counted on him to be the stable parent in both of their lives since their mother left.

"Not now, man," Aiden warned and nodded to the opened door. He knew Rose would see it as an invitation to personally spy on the two of them. She meant well, but sometimes he felt like a little boy again with the way she hovered. What he was doing in a BDSM club or the fact he acted like a complete ass to a perfectly lovely woman, wasn't something he wanted to share with the woman who was like a mother to him.

"Fine, but we aren't finished talking about what happened, Aiden. You need to get over being an ass. I'm sure the pretty woman from the club has already forgotten all about you," Corbin teased, again laughing at his own joke.

"What pretty girl from which club?" Rose asked, pushing her way into the room. Aiden groaned and Corbin seemed to find his discomfort even more amusing.

"Go ahead, man," Corbin taunted. "Tell mom how you fucked up and then I can be her favorite again."

Aiden shot him a look hopefully telling him to shut the fuck up but from the knowing smirk on his best friend's face, he didn't give a shit what Aiden wanted. "We both know you're Rose's favorite. I'm just your annoying best friend who you could never shake off," Aiden grumbled. He hoped he could change the topic, but when Rose put her hands on her hips and stared him down, he knew there would be no getting around her question.

"Focus, Aiden," she prompted. "Girl—night club?" she questioned.

He sighed, "Fine," he said. "I met a nice woman at a night club and I fucked things up with her and now I can't stop thinking about her or the way I screwed everything up," he admitted.

"Well, I'm sure it's not the first time you goofed things up with a pretty woman. Maybe you should cut yourself a break. It hasn't been very long since Allison left you and the girls. You should take some time off dating and concentrate on your family. I know that working and your campaign are stressful, maybe you should hire someone to help out," Rose said. He wasn't sure how to explain to her that meeting women had nothing to do with dating right now and everything to do with fucking. Corbin smiled over at him, standing in the corner of his office, as if trying to stay out of the way.

"You," he shouted, pointing at Corbin, "need to mind your own fucking business. And, as for the extra help, I have all I can possibly handle. The company is running as smoothly as possible with Corbin taking over some of my case load and my fantastic assistant having my schedule nailed down to the very last second for me. My campaign is going well and I have excellent staff on that end. Hell, they've completely covered up the fact my wife left me. As far as anyone is concerned, Allison is at home lovingly taking care of our family while I'm out winning votes. There hasn't been one single press leak about anything that has happened between the two of us. I signed the divorce papers and thought that would set off a frenzy in the press but nothing, nada—not that I'm complaining." His campaign was headed up by some of the area's best and he couldn't ask for a better campaign manager. Derrika Clayton was highly recommended and cost him a small fortune, but she knew how to put out fires before they were even an ember and he had to admit he was damn thankful for her. His biggest problem was keeping his new social life private and out of the public eye. If anyone found out he had covered up the fact he and his so called devoted wife were in fact divorced, his whole campaign would be over. He needed to just hang in there a little while longer and then he'd be able to announce his wife had left him and he was trying to pick up the pieces and be the best father he could be to his two little girls. Derrika just wanted to get past the primaries in a few weeks and then he could make the announcement and stop living under the deception that everything was fine. Honestly, he looked forward to the day he could announce to the world he was living a lie. Sneaking around and being under the public's microscope wasn't the kind of life he wanted for him or his daughters. Plenty of men were in his shoes and he was sure Derrika was making a bigger deal out of him being jilted by his ex-wife than she needed to. Still, he trusted her and she was his campaign manager. He'd do what she wanted, for now.

"I'm not talking about your staff at work or on the campaign, Aiden," Rose said, interrupting his thoughts. "I think it's time you hired a nanny to help with the girls. They hate coming here after daycare while you finish up with work. They're bored and need more stability then hanging out in your office while you try to make phone calls. They need someone who is going to take them to the park or arrange playdates with kids their age." Rose did have a point. Connie tried telling him the same thing a few weeks back. He was sure his ex-mother-in-law was trying to help but at the time, it felt like a criticism. Lately, Aiden felt as if he couldn't do a damn thing right and having Connie tell him he needed a nanny only seemed to drive home his point. If he hired outside help that would mean he wasn't doing a good enough job with his daughters and that was something he couldn't fuck up.

"No," he said. Rose nodded and started for the door, grabbing some files from his desk. He knew he upset her but he was being a stubborn ass.

"You should at least think about it, man," Corbin said. "Mom isn't trying to hurt your feelings or say you're fucking things up. We both see you are struggling and maybe hiring someone to help with the girls isn't such a bad idea." Rose stopped in the doorway to look back at him and he hated the hurt he saw in her eyes. Upsetting Rose was something he hated doing. Having her disappointed in him usually felt like a knife to the gut and he'd do just about anything to avoid hurting her. Aiden knew they were both right; hiring a nanny might be good for his girls. He also knew what he was currently doing wasn't what any of them needed. Lucy and Laney deserved more than he was giving them. They deserved his best and maybe the only way he could give that to them was to hire some help.

"Fine," he whispered. "Can you call some of the local agencies and start the process?" he asked. Rose nodded.

"I'll set up some interviews, weed out the ones who aren't a fit and pick a few for you to look at," she offered.

"Thanks, Rose," he said. She left his office, pulling the door shut behind her, leaving him with Corbin and what he knew was going to become a game of twenty questions. "Please don't start with me," he said, holding up his hands. "I'm spent and just want to get done my work and go home." Corbin's sympathetic look nearly pissed him off again. He could handle snarky and condescending from his best friend but pity or sympathy was another story.

"Don't look at me like that either," he said.

"How am I looking at you exactly, Aiden?" Corbin questioned.

"Like you pity me. I don't need that right now, Corbin," he said.

"I won't hide the fact I'm concerned for you, Aiden. That's what friends do or have you forgotten that?" Corbin asked. "You need to learn to let a few things go and stop beating yourself up every time you fuck things up."

"Yeah, I get that. But I didn't just fuck things up with Zara. I royally fucked things up. I overreacted and blew things way out of proportion. Hell, she seemed fine with the fact I took her virginity and I was the one acting like a catholic schoolgirl over the whole issue," Aiden admitted.

"Well, you can act like quite the drama queen, AJ," Corbin teased. "Have you thought about going back to the club and asking about her? They are members only and would have some record of her I'm sure." Honestly, finding Zara was all he could think about but then what? Once he had her information would he just casually call her up and ask how she was? Starting the phone conversation like, "Hey- it's me the guy who took your virginity and then yelled at you for no reason," didn't seem like a great plan.

Maybe it's best if you just forget about her, man," Corbin said. Aiden wished it was that simple. He wanted to push the sexy images of Zara from his mind. Remembering the way she looked up at him through her long lashes, watching his every move like she would never be able to get enough of him, wasn't something he would easily forget.

"I don't know," Aiden grumbled. "Right now I just want to finish up this file I'm working on, pick up my girls from Connie's place and head home. I have a six pack with my name on it."

"Now, that sounds like a fucking plan," Corbin said. "Just think about what I said, AJ. If you can't just forget her then find her and do a little groveling."

"As if you've ever begged a woman for anything," Aiden teased. It was true though. Corbin never had to work to get or keep a woman. It had even turned into a problem for him quite a few times when the woman refused to take no for an answer. Corbin wasn't the kind of guy who dated, really. He was a Dom who liked to work his way through subs. When the sub got the wrong idea and started to develop feelings for his friend, Corbin usually found an excuse to end the contract with the poor woman. Most of his subs took the news fine and found another Dom to play with at the club but some didn't like being so easily rejected. Aiden worried sooner or later Corbin was going to piss off the wrong woman and she'd take things too far, but his happy go lucky friend didn't seem too worried about the possibility of a disgruntled sub exacting her revenge.

"Yeah well, some of us are just gifted, I guess," Corbin teased. He walked out of Aiden's office, smiling back over his shoulder and Aiden chuckled. His friend was always a rule breaker, but he was pretty sure sooner or later, Corbin would meet a woman who would knock him on his ass. Aiden just hoped like hell he'd have front row seats to watch that show.

ZARA

Zara had spent two weeks trying to find a new job and she was worried nothing would ever pan out. The family she nannied for found out she ended up at the BDSM club and fired her. It didn't seem to matter to the woman she nannied for how her husband came by this information or that he was also a member of the club. Zara wanted to let the cat out of the bag but ruining a family wasn't her thing. Besides, she believed in karma and knew sooner or later his luck would run out.

She was just about to give up on the whole nanny gig when a new agency called her wanting to interview her for a potential high profile client. She was used to working with families who wanted their private lives kept private. Most of her clients consisted of high profile parents who were usually CEOs or involved in politics at some level. She knew how to keep her lips zipped on the playground while the other nannies droned on about the people they worked for. Zara learned to look the other way and just do her job and until a couple weeks ago, she never had any issues with the people she nannied for.

"Hey you," Avalon said as she came barreling through their front door. She and Ava had been roommates for almost five years now. Zara needed a place to live while she was still in college and she was lucky enough to become friends with her biology lab partner —Avalon Michaels. She and Ava instantly hit it off and when she offered to let her move into her townhouse, close to campus, Zara jumped at the offer. It was perfect really, she had her own room and bathroom and Ava's job, working for a clothing designer, had her working crazy hours and flying to fabulous places like Paris and Milan. Zara had the privacy she needed and when the people she nannied for would need her to spend the night, she could easily just pack a bag with the reassurance she'd have a place to stay when the job was over. Not every family wanted a live- in nanny. Most families just wanted her to stay over if the parents had a late night function to attend or just wanted to get away. Still, it was nice not to have an uptight roommate fussing over her not being home all the time. She and Ava were a roommate match made in heaven besides being best friends.

"Hey yourself," Zara said. "You need help with that?" She motioned to the giant suitcase Ava took with her on most of her trips.

"Nope," Ava said, tugging her luggage the rest of the way through the door. "This monstrosity and I have become one. She understands I need to buy everything in Paris and doesn't judge me." Ava patted her suitcase as if she were praising a puppy and set it off to the side.

"Um, I don't think your suitcase cares what you put in her," Zara teased.

"She doesn't mean it, baby," Ava said to her luggage in her sing- song voice. "Honestly Zara, you are no fun anymore."

"Yeah well, while you've been in Paris, I've been here pounding the pavement for a job. Your little dare cost me my job, Ava," Zara grouched.

"And I've apologized for that a gazillion times, Z," Ava said. "I feel horrible that happened, but how were either of us to know your boss would be there the same night as you. Hell, did you know he was into that type of thing?" Zara shrugged, not wanting to tell her best friend not only did she know he was into a whole lot of kink, but he had asked her to join him and his wife a few times; although she doubted his wife had any idea what was going on.

"I didn't even know I was into it until that night," Zara whispered under her breath. Ava apparently heard her, judging from her giggle.

"Well, you at least have that to take away, even if the rest of the night ended in disaster," Ava said.

"Sure," Zara agreed. "And a new agency just called and I have an interview tomorrow."

"That's fantastic," Ava offered. She crossed the room and pulled Zara in for a bear hug.

"Listen, I have a million things to do before tomorrow gets here. How about you unpack then show me all of the latest fashions you brought back from

Paris over dinner?" Zara had already started making a mental list of everything she needed to pick up for her interview before Ava even agreed.

"We meet back here at six and I'll order Chinese from our favorite place," Ava said. Zara love the way her best friend's good moods were almost infectious. She couldn't help her smile as she watched Ava tug her luggage up the stairs to her bedroom. She just hoped by this time tomorrow she'd be in a better mood after hopefully getting the job. She could use a win about now.

Zara spent the rest of the day getting ready for her job interview and then the evening eating noodles and listening to Ava go on about what everyone was wearing at fashion week in Paris. Her friend was born with a silver spoon in her mouth. Avalon's family was well known in the political arena. Her grandfather and father were both congressmen and even though Ava didn't usually act it, Zara knew she came from old money. Ava barely charged her any rent to live in the townhome they shared and she was always treating Zara to dinner and buying her little presents. It was quite different from the way Zara grew up. She lost her parents when she was just nine years old and was moved from foster home to foster home until she turned eighteen. When she finally got out of the system, she ran as far and fast as she could.

It was by chance she ended up at the local university.

She was working at a diner in town, waitressing to make ends meet and trying to afford the shitty little apartment she was living in. One night, the owner sat her down and told her she believed Zara could be more than just a waitress in a rundown diner and she handed her an application and a pamphlet with information about a scholarship she might qualify for. She got a full ride and was pursuing her degree in early childhood education until the scholarship's funds ran dry and she had to quit. She was one semester short of graduation and Ava insisted she let her pay but it just didn't feel right to take her money. It was something Zara wanted to do on her own, so she started fulfilling her credits class by class. She was enrolled in her last class starting in the fall and she honestly couldn't wait to walk across the stage and accept her diploma. She fought so hard for it, there would be no stopping her now.

Maybe not having family left was why she loved the way Ava so easily accepted her. Ava made sure she was never alone on holidays and her birthday. Up until her twentieth birthday, Zara hadn't really celebrated. After meeting Ava, she made sure Zara had a party every year to make up for all the missed birthdays.

"So, any word from BDSM guy?" Ava asked around a mouthful of noodles.

Zara rolled her eyes. Telling Ava about that night might have been a mistake but she didn't have anyone else to talk to. Hell, she made so many mistakes that night she wasn't sure which she regretted most. Not telling Aiden about her being a virgin rated right up at the top of her regrets list but she really wouldn't change much about the night. God, he was perfect the way he took complete control over her body, mind and soul. It was as if he could read her every need and gave her what she had been searching for. And just when she thought she was going to get everything she ever wanted, he pushed her away and went radio silent. Aiden asked to see her again but, that was before he found out she was a virgin. Zara couldn't blame him, really. She knew who she was—a twenty-five year old virgin and what man would want her? She was a fool to believe a man like Aiden would want someone like her. She was broken and naïve. A man like Aiden was looking for a real woman—one with experience and knowledge of how to pleasure a man. That wasn't her.

"No, and how would he reach me?" she whispered. "It isn't like we exchanged numbers or anything, Ava," she admitted. It was true. After Aiden made her feel like shit for omitting her sexual status, she grabbed her things and high- tailed it out of that club.

"You know I can get his information for you, right? I have a friend who works there, you know in security and I'm sure he'll do a little digging for me. Besides, he owes me," Ava admitted.

"Lord, do I want to know why he owes you a favor?" Zara teased.

"Well, I hooked him up with another friend and so far, so good. They've been going out for a few months now," Ava said. "So, how about it? Want me to track down your mystery man?"

She wanted to tell her friend yes but that would mean admitting to wanting Aiden and if she said those words out loud, Ava would never let her live any of this nightmare down. If it was up to Zara she would just forget the whole night even happened but that was proving nearly impossible. She was pretty sure she'd never be able to forget Aiden or the way he made her completely his even if it was for just one night.

Zara woke early the next morning and went for a run. She had a love/hate relationship with running and for some crazy reason, she just couldn't seem to give it up. Really it was one of the best ways she knew to relieve stress and right now, she had plenty of that. She quickly showered and threw on the outfit Ava helped her to pick out the night before. According to her best friend it was not only business sheik, but also screamed she wasn't afraid to get down and play with the kids, when she needed to. Honestly, it was fancier than most of the outfits she wore on a daily basis. Zara found kids really didn't care what she was wearing as long as she knew the way to the park and where to drop them off at their friend's houses after school, she was golden.

By the time she got to the address for the office building the agency had given to her, she was a full ten minutes early and pretty damn proud of herself for pulling that off. Actually her punctuality was one of her selling points and being early would help to drive that point home when she brought it up in casual conversation during the interview. She had a seat in the waiting area where the security guard told her to hang out and

ZARA

she wondered just whom she was interviewing with. The gold letters on the side of the building said Eklund and Bentley and she knew the woman conducting the interview was named Rose Eklund, so she assumed it was for that partner but that was all she had to go on.

A woman who looked to be probably somewhere in her mid-forties hurried towards her wearing a triumphant smile. It was hard not to return her kind gesture; it was almost infectious. "You must be Zara," the woman said, more stating a fact than asking. "I'm Rose Eklund and I will be interviewing you for Mr. Bentley." She looked Zara up and down and nodded as if happy with what she saw. "Please follow me," the kind woman said.

She led the way to the elevator and when it stopped, Zara couldn't help but admire the view. The top floor had an almost panoramic view of the city and she wondered if she could see her and Ava's place from where she stood. "Impressive, isn't it?" Rose asked, watching her reaction.

"Very," Zara agreed.

"Please have a seat and make yourself comfortable. Mr. Bentley couldn't be here today. He was called out of town on business but has left hiring a nanny for his two girls to me," Rose said.

"That is quite a responsibility," Zara admitted.

Rose smiled at her and nodded. "Well, the girls are like my grandchildren. I've known them their whole lives and practically raised their father. He and my son, Corbin are best friends and they own this business. So, it's really an honor to find a nanny for Lucy and Laney."

"And Mrs. Bentley?" Zara asked. One thing she learned working for high powered clients was what questions to ask and which to avoid. If she was going to be the family's nanny, she needed to know their dynamics. "Will she be joining us?"

"God, I hope not," Rose protested. "She left Mr. Bentley and the girls a little over half a year ago. She has very little contact with the girls. The last time any of us saw her was at Lucy's fifth birthday a few months back. Other than that, she has nothing to do with them."

Zara felt instantly sad for the little girls she didn't even know yet. She knew exactly what it felt like to be alone and wish for her mother, only to have the disappointment of knowing her mother would never be back. It broke her heart knowing a mother could just walk away from her own flesh and blood so easily.

"I'm sorry," she all but whispered.

"Nothing to be sorry for," Rose offered. "It was hard on everyone at first but we've all adapted. Mr. Bentley has a crazy schedule and is running for the vacant senate seat next fall, so his plate is full. He just needs a little help with the girls' schedules—you know to keep them on track."

"You said Lucy is just five. How old is Laney?" Zara asked.

"She will be three in a few months and she's a spit fire," Rose said, smiling to herself. "Do you mind if I ask you a few questions? The agency sent over your resume and it looks great, but I'm wondering why your last job ended so abruptly." Zara tried not to cringe but she must have given some sign of distress at Rose's question.

"Things didn't really work out. I'm not at liberty to say why, since I signed a non-disclosure agreement with my contract. It's really a matter of privacy, both mine and theirs." Rose watched her as if trying to read between the lines to pick up what she wasn't saying. "Let's just say I was in the wrong place at the wrong time," Zara offered. She hoped that would be enough of an explanation to get Rose to move onto the next question on her list but she wasn't exactly sure it was.

"Well, it's nice to hear you honor your former client's privacy even after you were let go. Your new agency has already vetted you, but are you willing to let us conduct our own background check, if we deem it necessary?" Rose asked. Zara nodded, not really having any skeletons in her closet—well, besides going into a BDSM club and having sex for the first time with a complete stranger. She just hoped their background check overlooked her latest indiscretion.

"Sure," she agreed.

"Great," Rose said. "Tell me why you became a nanny, Zara," she asked.

This was her favorite question to answer and also the toughest. She would always be truthful about her past, but sometimes families didn't like the fact she was raised in the foster care system. It was as if they thought she was somehow damaged. "My parents both died when I was very young and I have no other family. I was placed in the foster care system and bounced around a little bit. I've been working my way through college and honestly, being a nanny is right in line with my major," she said.

"Oh, and what is that?" Rose questioned.

"I'm majoring in early childhood education. I want to be a teacher. I have one more class to take in the fall and then I can graduate. But don't worry," she said. "My class is in the evening and work always comes first." Rose nodded again and checked her paper and then sat it back down on the desk.

"It must have been awful for you, growing up without parents. I'm sure they would be proud of the young woman you've become," Rose offered. Zara had always wondered if her mother and father would have approved of her choices and the path she had taken. They would have been so happy she was able to work her way through college, but she wondered if some of her other choices would make them proud. It wasn't something she let her thoughts linger on too long because focusing on them always made her heart ache a little. Sure, she had grown up and learned to live without either of them, but she would always wonder what if and that was a dangerous game to play.

"That is very kind of you to say, Rose," she whispered.

"Well, if you have no further questions for me, I'd like to know when you can start," Rose said. Zara all but stood from her chair, dumping the contents of her purse onto the floor.

"I'm so sorry," she muttered. Rose stood and helped her gather her things from the floor, handing her back her bag.

"No, it's fine. I'm always a bundle of nerves when it comes to these things myself. You might think it's nerve racking being on the interviewee side but interviewing someone is just as stressful. Maybe I didn't handle that right. I guess I should have asked if you'd like the job?" Rose waited her out and Zara wasn't sure if jumping up and down, clapping and cheering was the correct response but she didn't care.

"Thank you so much," she said. "I'd have to meet the family first but I think I'd love to take the job," she offered. "When would you like for me to start?"

"How about tomorrow morning, eight sound good? You can meet the girls, but their dad will be out of town for a few more days. We'll get you settled in before he even gets back," Rose said. Zara noticed a glint of mischief in the older woman's eyes and she wondered if it was going to turn out to be a good or bad thing for her.

"If you're sure that is alright, then yes. Tomorrow morning works for me," Zara admitted.

"Great. Will you have much to move in?" Rose asked.

"Move in?" Zara questioned. "I was told this wasn't a live-in role." The agencies she worked with usually gave her a heads up if the position required her to be a full time live-in nanny. She tried to avoid those jobs but she so desperately needed this one, she really didn't' have a choice.

"I'm sorry," Rose offered. "You will need to be there quite a bit during the campaign. I'm afraid the girls haven't' had much stability or structure lately. It would help them tremendously if you could be there for them twenty-four hours a day. You can have most weekends off, if you'd like." Zara knew she was going to have to make a quick decision, but the idea of leaving Ava high and dry for the unforeseeable future made her feel bad. She also knew if she wanted to finish her last semester of school, she was going to have to have a job to pay her tuition bill.

"Yes," Zara agreed, holding out her hand to shake on it. "I'll take the job and I'll move into their home. It will be on a trial basis, of course."

"Of course," Rose agreed, shaking her hand. "We can re-evaluate when the election is over, if that works for you." Zara nodded. "Great." Rose pulled a slip of paper out and handed it to her. "Be at this address by eight tomorrow and bring whatever you will need for the time being. If you need to hire a moving crew, just send me the bill and I'll take care of it for you." Rose walked to the elevator and Zara followed.

"Thank you," Zara said.

"No, thank you," Rose returned. "I hope you like a little chaos because you're about to dive in, headfirst." Zara wanted to laugh at what she thought was a joke but judging from the expression on Rose's face, she wasn't joking.

AIDEN

Spending half a week in boardrooms and one boring meeting after another, Aiden was ready to get home and sink into his own bed. He was just thankful he was able to slip away from his trip two days early because spending one more day away from his girls was going to drive him crazy. Corbin had been handling the business trips since Allison left but he couldn't say no to this one. This trip involved a company that was his baby from the start and he needed to be involved in the negotiations. Sending Corbin in his stead felt wrong and he was glad he made that decision because he had to put out some major fires.

Aiden unloaded his luggage into the corner of the mudroom, deciding he'd deal with it all tomorrow. Tonight, he wanted to peek in on his girls and meet the new nanny Rose hired. She was supposedly staying in his guest room and he wasn't sure how he felt about having a live-in nanny. The press might catch wind of it and have a field day with the news. But, Rose assured him his new nanny wouldn't cause him any trouble and as far as looks went, she described her as frumpy and easily overlooked. Aiden just hoped Rose was right because he didn't have time to squash rumors about his new help.

He checked in on the girls to find them both peacefully sleeping and made his way down to the spare room Rose said she put the new nanny in but he found the room empty. He decided to search for her, hoping she wouldn't just leave the girls alone, when he heard water running in his bathroom. What the hell was the nanny doing in his master bathroom?

"Hello?" he called and no one answered. He rounded the corner and found the door to his bathroom closed. "Hello," he said, banging on the door. No one answered and he had no choice but to try the doorknob hoping his new nanny was decent but not really giving a shit at this point. First he'd introduce himself and then he was going to lay down a few ground rules; the first being no using his master bath. The second would be to answer the fucking door when he knocked, but he was sure barging in on her would solve that little problem.

"Hi," he said to the back of the blonde head that greeted him. The woman in the tub full of bubbles didn't answer him and he was beyond frustrated by her complete lack of attention. What if it had been one of his girls who needed her? "Hello," he shouted, going the extra mile to tap her on her shoulder. He tried to ignore the way the bubbles enveloped her sexy curves or the fact she was a whole fucking lot younger than Rose had described her and one hundred percent sexier. He made a mental note to have a little chat with Rose about how she described people and her use of adjectives, the next time he saw her. His new nanny was neither frumpy nor old. In fact she was damn sexy.

As soon as he tapped her shoulder, she squealed and jumped, pulling her earbuds from her ears. "Sorry," she stuttered, looking him over. "Oh fuck," she swore. "Aiden?" He stood over the tub and realized the woman staring back at him was the same woman he had been dreaming about for the past few weeks, the one he couldn't seem to forget—Zara.

"What the hell are you doing in my house, Zara?" he questioned. She stood from the soapy water, letting the bubbles slide down her curves and he couldn't seem to take his eyes off her. He was immediately reminded of their night together, her breathy sighs and the way she shouted his name when she came on his tongue. And now, she stood completely bare in his tub and all he could think about was how she ended up there.

"Your home?" she questioned. "Wait—you are Mr. Bentley? Lucy and Laney are your daughters?" Zara questioned. He slowly nodded, trying to catch up.

"Yes," he said. He handed her a towel knowing if she continued to stand in front of him completely naked, he might not be able to regain cognitive thought clear enough to keep up with his end of the conversation. "Can you please wrap this around yourself?" he asked. She shot him a look that told him she wasn't in the same submissive mood she was in the night they shared together.

What, Aiden," she spat, snatching the towel from his

hand, "my naked body offends you now?" He couldn't take his eyes off her as Zara wrapped the towel around her wet body and he felt about ready to swallow his tongue. "My body didn't seem to bother you that night in the club," she spat. God, she was gorgeous and he had to fight every one of his natural instincts to pull her against his body and make her his again. But, she wasn't his—she never was his and he needed to remember that.

"That was before you were my nanny, Zara. So, you didn't know the job was for me?" he questioned. He hated how he sounded, like he was accusing her of something but he couldn't help it. If there was any chance she was stalking him or his girls were in danger, he would do what ever it took to make them safe.

"Of course I didn't," she insisted. "Why would I take this job knowing you will be my boss. As far as I'm concerned we said everything we needed to say that night. If I remember correctly, you accused me of lying and I ran out of the club half naked and completely ashamed. Thanks for that, by the way," she said. He hated hearing he made her feel that way. It wasn't what he intended and he had spent the last few weeks feeling like a complete ass for what he said to her.

"I'm sorry for that, Zara," he admitted. "I handled taking your virginity all wrong and I regret the way things ended that night." She stepped from the tub, pulling the drain and brushed past him to leave the bathroom. She smelled like flowers and he knew for a fact she tasted like honey. Just the thought of her scent and taste made his mouth water and his cock spring to life. He wanted to push her against the fucking wall and kiss her until they were both breathless and needy but he could tell that was something she wouldn't allow. So, he let her pass and followed her down the hall to her bedroom.

Aiden stood helplessly in her doorway, watching as the woman who occupied his every waking and sleeping hours pulled on a pair of yoga pants and a t shirt, forgoing undergarments. "Listen, I'll be out of your hair by morning," she said. Zara was shoving clothing into a bag and he felt a moment of panic, not knowing if he should feel relief she was going to leave or fear he was going to have to watch her walk away again and possibly this time forever.

"So that's it? You're just going to walk away and leave the girls?" Aiden asked. He hated the idea of his daughters having to lose someone they were getting close to again. The past few nights, when he called home to talk to Lucy and Laney, they seemed so happy about the new nanny. They called her "Z" and Aiden just never put two and two together and why would he? Aiden would have never guessed Zara would not only show up in his life again, but as his daughters' nanny—it was just too much of a crazy coincidence.

"Well, I certainly can't keep working for you—not now, knowing that it's you," she said. She motioned to him as if trying to prove a point and he almost wanted to laugh at her grand, sweeping hand gestures.

"Listen," he started. Aiden knew he had to be patient if he was going to have any chance of talking her into staying with them. Hell, he wasn't sure what he wanted exactly but he knew letting her go would only hurt his

AIDEN

girls. "My daughters have been through hell this year. Their mother walked away from them and has very little contact with any of us since the divorce was finalized."

Zara looked down at the clothes she was holding and dropped them to her bed. "I know," she admitted. "Rose told me some of it and the girls still talk about her. I'm so sorry you three had to go through all of that but I still don't think me being here is a good idea," she said.

"How about if we can work out some kind of agreement? You know, I'll keep my distance and give you some space and you just take care of my girls?" he asked. He sounded more like he was begging but he didn't give a fuck. His daughters were worth any amount of begging he had to do to keep them happy.

"Why would you want me around, Aiden?" Zara questioned.

There really wasn't a clear cut explanation as to why he wanted to keep her around. Aiden knew part of it was the fact he liked seeing her again. Even in his wildest dreams, he never imagined he'd find Zara naked and wet in his bathtub after he returned from his business trip. He wasn't about to look a gift horse in the mouth though and keeping Zara around just felt like the right thing to do.

"The past few nights, when I've spoken with Lucy and Laney, they both seemed so happy. They went on and on about their new friend, Z and I have to admit it was nice to hear my girls sound excited about something again. It's been months since I've heard either of them sound so happy. I don't know—it was nice to hear. I worried less about being away from either of them, knowing you were here. Well, not you exactly but someone they were both coming to trust. If you leave now, they might never trust anyone to come into our home to take care of them again. Please," he begged.

Zara sat down on her bed next to the pile of clothes she had been working on. "You really know how to work the whole sympathy factor, don't you?" she asked. "I do love your girls. I have to admit in just a few short days, they've really grown on me." She smiled and then broke out into full giggles and Aiden couldn't help himself, he found himself chuckling right along with her.

"Mind sharing what's so funny?" he asked.

"Well, Lucy was telling me her daddy was flying like Superman and he had a red cape and everything. You know she really believes you're a superhero? I guess I was just picturing you in a Superman costume," she admitted. She looked Aiden up and down and then broke out in a fit of giggles, falling back onto the bed.

Aiden flexed his muscles, as if trying to show off for her but that only sent her further over the edge. "Is it really so hard to believe I could be a superhero?" he asked. Sure, saying the words aloud made him sound crazy but he had to admit his feelings were a little hurt.

Zara seemed to sober at his lack of hysteria, picking up on the signs he didn't find the whole thing as funny as she had. "I think it's nice your daughters think of you in that way," she admitted. "I'm sure I felt the same way about my dad, when he was alive," she almost whispered that last part.

"I'm sorry," Aiden offered. "How old were you when he died?" he questioned. He wasn't sure if her personal life was any of his business, but a part of him hoped she would want to share something like that with him.

"When I was nine," she said. "Both of my parents died in a car crash. They were hit by a drunk driver." Aiden saw the sadness in her eyes and heard every ounce of her heartbreak in her shaky voice. He wished he wasn't dredging up such bad memories for her but a part of him wanted to know more about his new nanny. Hell, he wanted to know everything she'd be willing to share with him but he wouldn't admit that to her. Telling Zara that might just scare her away and he couldn't let that happen.

"That must have been horrible for you, Zara," he said. Aiden crossed the small bedroom and pushed some of her clothes aside to sit next to her on the bed. He worried about crossing some imaginary line, but when she didn't balk at the idea of him sitting so close to her, he didn't make a move to get up. "What happened to you after they died?" he asked.

Zara sighed, "Well, I was placed in foster care and bounced from place to place," she admitted.

"Shit," he swore. "That sucks."

"No, really it wasn't as bad as you might think. I was lucky enough to be placed with decent families," she said. "You hear horror stories about kids who are abused in some form or another but I got through the system unscathed and I believe I'm a stronger person for the time I was in there. It made me want to become a teacher and taught me to fight for what I want." Aiden took her hand into his, needing the contact. He knew it was silly; he just promised to give her space but none of that mattered at the current moment.

"I'm in college and I have one more class to take and then I graduate. Working as a nanny was supposed to be a part- time gig and give me some extra experience on my resume for after college. But, it became so much more than that. I've grown to love the kids I work with and I honestly find the work fulfilling," she said. Zara paused and Aiden wasn't sure if she was finished talking or if she was going to say what was on her mind.

"Listen, if this is all too much for you, just say the word and I'll have the agency place me with another family," she said. A pang of jealousy ran through him and Aiden shook it off. He had no claim to her professionally or personally, so he had no right to feel that way. The idea of Zara with any family but his own made him inexplicably grumpy.

"No," he said. "I'd like for you to stay. The girls seem to be crazy about you and I promise to keep my distance." Zara looked down to where their hands were joined and smiled.

"Um," she said, holding up their linked fingers, as if trying to prove her point.

"Yeah," he said, letting go of her hand. "Sorry about that." Aiden felt anything but sorry but he was going to keep that to himself. "How about we say that rule starts now?" he asked. Zara smiled and nodded. A strand of her long blonde hair fell from her messy bun and he wanted to reach over and tuck it back but he didn't. He was going to have to make an effort to keep his hands to himself but he'd do just that if it meant keeping Zara on. Maybe he was a masochist and having to deal with the realization of having Zara under his roof, but not being able to touch her was just the type of torture he was in to.

Zara stretched and yawned and he let his eyes lazily roam her body. Yeah, he was definitely a masochist. There was no other explanation for the self-torture he was putting himself through. "How about I let you get some sleep. I'll get up with the girls in the morning and see them off to school. You take the morning off—maybe sleep in. I'd like to spend some time with Lucy and Laney since this was the first trip I've taken since their mom left."

"Thank you," she said.

"Sure. Will you be free tomorrow for lunch?" he asked. He could see the way she suspiciously watched him and he worried she was getting the wrong idea. "For a work meeting," he amended. "We need to go over schedules and house rules, if this arrangement will work," he said.

Zara seemed to hesitate and then agreed. "Yes, that might be best. Besides, I have to return a few books I borrowed from Rose." Aiden wondered what books Zara had borrowed but he was sure he wasn't going to like her answer. Rose was constantly reading those sappy romance novels and the idea of Zara reading them made him a little hot. The less he thought about his new nanny reading steamy sex scenes from a novel the better.

He stood and crossed the room. "How about noon?" he asked. Zara nodded and he took that as his cue to leave. He was just about to his room when he heard her soft string of curses and he smiled to himself. Zara had just summed up exactly how he felt about finding out she was his daughters' new nanny, but for the first time in weeks, he was looking forward to the next day.

ZARA

Zara slept until just after seven and when she couldn't sleep anymore, she got up, dressed and ate breakfast. It felt strange being in the house by herself especially now that she knew it belonged to Aiden. She had just enough time to run over to Ava's to pick up the rest of her things and meet Aiden at his office for lunch. He left her a note letting her know they would have to have lunch delivered to his office because his schedule was packed for the day. That was fine with her because it would give her an excuse to leave to finish unpacking before the girls needed to be picked up from pre-school.

Lucy would probably try to coax her into going to the park on their way home and honestly, she loved the idea. Being outside always seemed like a good thing and after the restless night she just had some fresh air might do her some good. Finding out Aiden was her new employer really threw her for a loop. Having him walk in to find her naked and soaking in a bubble bath in his master bathroom wasn't her finest moment. Really, she shouldn't be embarrassed given the fact he had already seen every square inch of her, up close and personally. But that didn't stop her from feeling awkward about the whole thing. When Aiden insisted she stay on to nanny the girls, she was relieved. Zara wasn't sure her new agency would be so willing to find her a new family to work for. She knew she was under a microscope, being the new girl and she wasn't sure how to explain how she met her new boss. The idea of having to tell anyone about her connection with Aiden made her want to crawl under a rock to hide.

She pulled up to the townhouse she and Ava shared and wondered if her best friend was still angry with her. When she announced she not only got the job but had to move in with the family, Ava was upset. It didn't matter that Zara told her the situation was only temporary, Ava hated the idea of not being roommates anymore. When the small moving company Rose hired showed up to pack and move her meager belongings, Ava left the townhouse in a huff and didn't even bother to say goodbye. Zara called and left a few messages for her but she knew in time, Ava would come around. Zara just hoped it would be sooner rather than later because she could really use her best friend to talk to now.

When she saw Ava's car was still in its spot, Zara felt a sense of relief knowing she was going to get her chance to make things right with her. She knew Ava couldn't resist some good gossip and Zara was about to deliver big time, once she shared the news of her new employer being the same man who took her virginity.

"Ava," she called through the house and received no

answer. She smiled knowing she'd probably find her friend still in her bed and once she heard Zara calling for her, she'd cover her head with her quilt and play opossum. Zara made her way to the second floor and found just what she expected—Ava covered like a giant lump, lying in the middle of her bed as still as could be. Zara couldn't' help her giggle.

"Hmm- I guess you're sleeping then and don't want the juicy gossip I've come to deliver," she taunted. Zara knew Ava would never be able to pass up gossip. Her friend was the type of woman who lived for that kind of thing and the juicier, the better.

Ava threw down her covers revealing her scantily clad body and Zara knew she had her on the hook. "Gossip?" Ava questioned. "You better not be fucking around with me, Zara. I'm still mad at you for ditching me to live with your new family," Ava warned.

Zara couldn't help but roll her eyes, "You know that's work, Ava. I really have no choice. Besides, this isn't the first time I've had to live with a family."

"Right but those other times were just for a night or two, when both parents had to go out of town. This time, you're moving out indefinitely and I hate it," Ava grouched.

Zara sat down on her bed, "I know but I need this job, Ava. If I want to finish my last semester at school, I need a way to pay for it. Besides, I already told you it's not forever. The man I'm working for is running for political office and as soon as the campaign is over, I will have the option to stay as a live-in nanny or move back in here," she said.

"And, you'll choose to move back in here—right?" Ava prodded. Zara smiled at her bossy best friend. Ava was used to getting her way in everything. She was a strong woman who would never understand Zara's desire to be submissive to a man. In fact, the idea of Ava being submissive to anyone was laughable.

"I promise to run everything by you before I make a decision," Zara said, crossing her heart for good measure.

"Alright," Ava breathed. "I'll forgive you for now. I reserve the right to be angry again at you later, if you choose to stay with that family," she said. "Now, spill your juicy gossip." Zara giggled and pulled Ava in for a quick hug.

"I think you're really forgiving me for the gossip but I'll take the win," Zara teased, releasing her friend. She stood and began to pace, not sure Ava was going to be at all happy about what she was about to admit. "I'm working for Aiden," she blurted out. She wanted to lead up to that point; tell Ava the story of how Lucy spilled her drink all over the both of them and she had to give the girls baths and the way they talked her into bubble baths in their dad's big tub. By the time she got Lucy and Laney to bed, all she could think about was sinking into a tub full of bubbles herself, never suspecting Aiden was her new boss or he'd be home early from his trip. He was supposed to be gone for another two nights, according to Rose.

She gave Ava a second to catch up and judging from the confusion clouding her friend's eyes, she might need some extra time. "Wait—what?" Ava got out of the bed and stood in front of Zara, effectively stopping her pacing. "Aiden, the guy from the BDSM club—he's your new boss?"

"Yep," Zara said.

"What the actual fuck, Z?" Ava shouted. Yeah, her friend was definitely not taking this well. "Start explaining," Ava ordered.

"Well, I told you I was called by the agency to work for a high profile family?" Zara asked.

Ava nodded, "Yes but you never said who it was for."

"I didn't know who it was for until last night when Aiden got home from his business trip and surprised me while I was soaking in his bathtub." Zara grimaced, knowing she should have left the part of Aiden finding her naked in the tub out of her story.

"Fuck," Ava spat. "So, you're working for Aiden Bentley? He's running for my grandfather's vacant Senate seat," Ava said. Zara really didn't follow politics, but she did remember Rose telling her "Mr. Bentley" was running for political office. "You didn't know your Aiden was running for Congress when you hooked up with him?" Ava questioned.

"First, he's not my Aiden. Second, we really didn't do much talking that night. He didn't ask questions and neither did I," Zara admitted. She knew that made her sound like a complete slut, but she wouldn't be ashamed of what happened that night between the two of them. Zara wanted to lose her virginity and try something new and Aiden unknowingly gave that to her.

"Is he married?" Ava questioned.

"I can't discuss that," Zara said. She knew she had to

be careful about what she told Ava. According to Rose, the press still hadn't gotten wind of Allison leaving him and the girls and his political advisors wanted to keep it that way. Zara had signed the disclosure stating she would not talk about Aiden or his family to anyone and she was sure that included her best friend.

"What do you mean by that? It's a simple question to answer, Z. Either he is or he isn't," Ava sassed.

"It's not that I can't answer the question because I don't know the answer, Ava. I signed something saying I can't discuss Aiden or his family with anyone—including you. Had I known it was Aiden, I wouldn't have signed that damn form because I need to talk to someone about all of this. I feel as if I'm going to lose my mind if I don't, but I need to make sure I'm not breaking my contract if I tell you everything."

"So you came all the way over here just to tell me you're working for Aiden Bentley and you can't spill any of the details?" Ava asked.

"Right," Zara agreed. "And, I need to ask you not to talk to anyone about anything I've told you prior to today about Aiden. I didn't work for him when our night together happened, but I'm sure that will fall under the agreement I signed, now that I am his girls' nanny." Ava gave a look that told her she found the whole thing as crazy as Zara did. She still wasn't sure how the hell this all happened but it had and she needed to protect herself and the girls. They were both innocent in all of this and that was the main reason she agreed to stay on.

"You can't continue to work for him. You know that,

right Z?" Ava questioned. The logical side of her knew it was an awful idea to continue to work for Aiden but her heart was the one leading the stampede right over the cliff. She had already developed a soft spot for Lucy and Laney over the past half a week. Every time they talked about their mother, she felt the same pangs of sadness remembering what losing her own mother felt like. Leaving them now would hurt the girls and she wouldn't do that to them.

"Aiden and I have an agreement. I'll stay on for the girls and he'll keep his distance," she said.

Ava barked out her laugh, "You know that sounds completely nuts, right?" she asked. Zara did, especially after hearing herself say it out loud.

"I know," she admitted. "I have no good explanation for any of this other than I can't leave the girls—they need me. They deserve someone stable in their lives and I might just be their only hope."

Ava pulled her in for another hug, "You are such a good person, Z," she whispered. "Just don't go and lose your heart to a bastard like Aiden Bentley. Remember how he treated you that night at the club. You deserve better than a man who could so easily cast you aside based on the status of your virginity." Ava was right and Zara knew she deserved a man who would love her no matter what but that wasn't what Aiden had agreed to. When he met her at the club, she made him the offer of her body—not her heart but she'd never share that information with Ava. She hated that was all she was willing to give to any man right now—her body. Zara needed her heart intact for now and she didn't have time for anything as silly as romance or love. She had to finish college and keep her head on straight or else everything she had worked so hard for would be for nothing.

"Don't worry, Ava. I can handle myself with Aiden," she promised. Zara just hoped she wasn't fooling both of them because her next stop was the sexy Dom's office and with the way he looked at her last night they were both going to have trouble keeping their distance from each other.

Ava helped Zara finish packing up her things and promised to keep her room open and ready for Zara's return. They said a tearful goodbye, which was completely unnecessary given the fact she was only going to be ten minutes across town, and Zara left for her meeting with Aiden. She hoped he'd be in a better mood today than he was last night after finding her using his personal bathroom. Zara needed to get a few things off her chest and it would be easier to do if Aiden was the suave, sweet man she met when she first entered the club.

She stepped off the elevator and was greeted by Rose's smiling face as soon as the doors opened. "Hey there, Zara," she said.

"Rose," Zara greeted. "Is he in?" She looked around the top floor where she had her interview a few days prior and wondered at just how much had changed in such a short time span.

"He is," Rose said. "Listen Zara, I had no idea you knew Aiden when I hired you." Zara was worried Aiden had come to his senses and sent Rose to fire her. It made sense; Rose was the one to hire her so why not let her be the one to fire her too?

"Please don't fire me," Zara begged. She knew she sounded desperate but she was. Not only did she need this job to finish college but she wanted to stay on for Lucy and Laney. "I didn't know Aiden was going to be my boss when you hired me," she admitted.

"I know you didn't and no one is getting fired," Rose soothed. She started down the hallway and stopped in front of what Zara assumed was Aiden's office door.

"Um, how much do you know?" Zara questioned.

"Know?" Rose asked.

"Yeah, about me?" Zara hesitantly asked. "What has Aiden told you?" She almost didn't want to know but she wouldn't hide from the truth. Zara wasn't ashamed of what happened but she hoped Aiden didn't share all the details of their night together. "You said you were close to him, like a mother figure," Zara reminded her.

"It's true that Aiden is like a son to me but he doesn't share his personal life easily. He told me you and he went on one date together but that was about it," Rose said. Hearing that Aiden didn't share all the sorted details about the club and the way he took control of her body, taking care of her every need; that had to count for something.

"If something happened between the two of you, it's none of my business. My only concern here is that you take care of Lucy and Laney. Aiden has been working so hard lately, he really needs the help," Rose admitted.

"Well, I will do my very best," she promised. "Thank you, Rose," Zara awkwardly pulled the older woman in for a quick hug.

"He said to send you in when you got here," Rose said. "I've cleared his schedule for the rest of the day and I'll make sure you're not interrupted." Zara nodded and took a deep breath, trying to steady her nerves before having to face her new boss.

"It's now or never," she breathed and turned the doorknob to walk into his office.

"Good luck, Dear," Rose whispered. Zara had a feeling she was going to need a whole hell of a lot more than luck. She was going to need a damn miracle to get through her meeting with Aiden.

AIDEN

Aiden looked up to find Zara walking into his office and he knew his time for hiding was over. He had been waiting all morning for their meeting. He'd like to say he was patiently waiting for his new nanny but that would be a complete lie. When he demanded the meeting, it was to lay down some house rules and hopefully set some boundaries—mostly for himself but partially for Zara. If this thing was going to work, the two of them would have to come to some understanding. His girls were too important not to try to work through the baggage between him and Zara, but seeing her last night naked in his tub made him want her all over again. Zara was a beautiful woman but there was something else—something that inexplicably drew him to her. They needed to get everything out into the open and hopefully find a way forward for Lucy and Laney's sake.

"I hope it's okay I just came in. Rose said you were waiting for me," Zara said. She seemed so unsure of herself and he hated making her feel that way. He stood and crossed his office to meet her, wanting to soothe her, make her feel some ease around him.

"No, it's fine," he offered, shutting the door behind her. "Please come in." He put his hand on the small of her back ushering her into his office, loving the way she shivered at his touch. He needed to keep his focus because eliciting any reaction from her wasn't what their meeting was about.

"Please have a seat," he said, nodding to the leather sectional that took up most of the corner of his office. "Can I get you something to drink?" he asked.

"No, thank you," she said. "I just came from my townhome, picking up the last of my things. I need to get back to your house, unpack and pick the girls up from school."

"Right," he whispered. So, she wanted to get right down to it and that worked for him. He didn't want to draw this out and make things worse than they needed to be. He was already nervous enough about this little chat. "I'm sorry about walking in on you last night. I didn't know you were naked; you know—when I came home."

Zara shrugged, "How could you? I didn't expect anyone home for two more nights," she admitted. "The girls wanted bubble baths in the big tub and I didn't know it would be such a big deal. It won't happen again," she promised.

"No, it's not a problem. The girls love my tub. They call it their swimming pool," he admitted. Zara giggled and it sounded like magic.

"That must have been what they were talking about

when they told me to watch out for the shark," she teased.

"Yeah," he laughed. "They both have big imaginations," he said. "Once, they told me they were mermaids and the mean pirates were trying to get them. I was trying to figure out what they were talking about and then I realized their grandmother, Connie was reading Peter Pan to them."

"I met her," Zara said. "She seems nice."

Aiden nodded, "She's been great. I wouldn't have been able to make it through the past half a year without her," he admitted.

Zara sat back against the back of the sofa, seeming a little more comfortable with him. "What are we going to do about our night at the club?" she asked.

"What do you mean by, 'do'?" he questioned.

"Well, do we just forget it happened or what?" she asked. The last fucking thing he wanted to do was forget it happened. He wanted her still and forgetting about their night together wasn't something he thought he'd ever be able to do.

"No," he breathed. "I don't want to forget that night," he admitted.

"Good," she said. "Me either. But I don't want it to affect me working for you. It happened and I don't regret making the decision to go back to your room with you. I am sorry I wasn't completely truthful though. I should have told you I was a virgin." She looked down at her hands that were fidgeting with her jacket and he hated they were back to her being nervous around him again.

AIDEN

"Look at me, Zara," he commanded. He knew he was taking a chance demanding anything from her but he couldn't help it. There was something about Zara that made him want to slip into full Dom mode. Her gorgeous blue eyes darted up to meet his own as she obeyed his order.

"I shouldn't have gotten so angry," he whispered. "I hate the way we left things and I shouldn't have yelled at you."

"But—" she stuttered.

"But nothing," he said. "You did nothing wrong. I should have asked more questions and gotten to know you a little more. I went about things all wrong and that's on me. You didn't do anything wrong. You were perfect," he whispered, pulling her body against his own. "You are perfect," he murmured against her lips. He didn't ask permission because he wasn't willing to wait for her answer. He needed her—now and waiting wasn't an option. He kissed her with all the pent-up desire he had felt for her over the past few weeks and Zara didn't seem to hold back with him either.

Aiden broke the kiss, leaving them both breathless and he wondered if he had just made a mistake, but judging from the desire he saw staring back at him in Zara's eyes, he hadn't. She seemed just as turned on by what was happening between the two of them as he was. Still, he waited, almost as if he was holding his breath, waiting for her to respond to him being so forward. Zara gave him no indication whether she was pissed but he knew better than to push.

"Tell me I overstepped, Zara," he demanded. "Slap

me, get mad at me but for God sake, do something. I need a sign here," he admitted, running his fingers through his own hair.

"I'm not angry with you, Aiden. I know I should be but I'm not. I'm not ashamed of what happened between us at the club. I wanted you then and I want you now, even if it is an awful idea. I mean, I'm your nanny—your employee." Hearing Zara call herself his employee made him want to laugh. He'd never slept with any of his employees, ever. It was just a personal rule that saved him a lot of trouble and probably kept his HR department happy. Corbin kept them busy enough with the way he seemed to like to sleep his way through his private assistants. He couldn't seem to keep his hands off them and Aiden had even threatened to give him Rose as his assistant, just to keep him in line. That always won him a round of groans from both Corbin and Rose, but he was at his wits end with his business partner not keeping it in his pants. He wondered if breaking his policy of no sex with employees was risky or if it was crazy enough to work. Aiden knew his wanting Zara wasn't going to just disappear. The past three weeks had proven that.

"The employee problem is only the tip of the iceberg for me. As far as the political world is concerned, I'm still happily married to Allison. My campaign manager has put on quite a show and I've agreed to stick with the ruse until the primaries are over. After that, I can make an announcement we split, but I've been given strict orders not to rock the boat. If news about whatever this is between us gets out, I can kiss my run for the Senate goodbye," he admitted. Aiden knew he sounded like a complete ass and maybe he was. He worked too hard and sacrificed everything to get where he was. He had hired the best team to get him into office and not listening to them might be career suicide.

"So, you are telling me anything that would happen between us would be a secret?" she questioned.

"I would never ask you to be my secret, Zara," he whispered.

"I appreciate that, Aiden. I want you and if that is the only way I can have you; I'll take it." Zara sat back, as if waiting him out and he knew what his answer was going to be before he even gave it. He wanted her and there would be no way to deny that. Not having her felt like a denial and he was sick and tired of not having anything his way. Zara would be the one thing he could do for himself.

"You need to be sure about this, Zara. If this doesn't work out between us, my girls will be the one to pay the price," Aiden whispered. "I can't let that happen."

"No, you are right, Aiden. We can't let the girls get caught up in the middle of whatever this is or will become," she agreed. "How do we keep them safe?" Aiden stood and paced the floor. He must have looked as if he was having a debate with himself. When Zara looked as if she wanted to chuckle, he shot her a look that had her thinking better of it.

"One of the reasons I was going to the club was for anonymity. But, that's becoming harder to assure as my campaign grows. My ex didn't share my need for kink. Hell, she was as straight- laced as they came when it came to sex. I guess that's why I started going to the club in the first place—you know to explore that side of myself after the divorce." Zara nodded. He wasn't really sure where he was going with all of this. He was probably just spilling his guts, but he wanted to know if he and Zara were even on the same page, before asking her for what he wanted.

"I'm sorry, Aiden. The divorce must have been hard on you, especially if you weren't allowed to talk about it with anyone," she said.

"I've had Rose and her son, Corbin is my best friend and business partner. They know and I can tell them anything. But yes, having only a handful of people to talk to has been hard on me and the girls. That's why I have to be careful with our next move. Did you like everything you saw that night at the club?" he questioned.

Zara didn't even hesitate with her answer. "Yes," she breathed.

"Was that your first time—you know in a BDSM club?" he asked. He knew it was her first time having sex, but he wondered if she had ever experienced any part of the kinky lifestyle or if their night together was one of many firsts for her. She shyly nodded her head.

"Yes," she whispered.

He couldn't help himself, he had to ask the next question even if he might not like her answer. "Did you like what we did together?"

Zara sighed and nodded. "I loved everything up until the point where—well, you know," she said.

"To the point where I acted like an ass and got mad

at you?" he asked. Zara nodded again and he wasn't sure what his next move should be. He knew what he wanted to do—push her down onto his sofa and strip her bare but that wouldn't get them to the place where they needed to be. If she was going to be his girls' nanny, he had to tread lightly and not bully his way through this part with Zara.

"I'm sorry for that, Zara. What I guess I want to know is if you'd be willing to explore that lifestyle with me. Again, everything that happens will have to be kept in confidence and we have to protect the girls at all costs. Would you be willing to try?" Aiden sat back down next to her and waited her out. He wanted her to agree but only if it was something she wanted.

"What are you proposing exactly?" she asked.

"Be my sub," he asked. Hell, it sounded more like a command but he didn't care. He wanted her to agree but he wouldn't push her.

"Your sub?" she questioned.

"Yes," he said. "It would play out like many of the scenes in the club. We would play and when you are in my bed, you will obey my commands." Just the thought of having complete control of Zara's body made him instantly hard.

"What about when we aren't in your bedroom, Aiden?" she asked.

"You will strictly be my employee, nothing more." He knew that sounded harsh but it was all he could give her right now. "As far as the rest of the world will know, you are just my girls' nanny and I'm still happily married to Allison. That can't change until things settle down with my campaign and then we can re-evaluate things."

"If I agree to this, I won't be able to tell anyone, will I?" Zara questioned.

"No," he confirmed. "No one will be able to know about us," he said.

"Can I think about it?" she whispered. His heart sank when she didn't agree with his requests. Aiden wasn't used to people telling him no. He needed to remember Zara wasn't outright turning him down, just asking for time to get her head straight. It was a good thing, really. He wanted her to enter this arrangement with both eyes open.

"Fine," he said. "But just know if you agree to this, you agree to everything. I can't jeopardize my run for office or my company and I won't hurt my daughters. This stays between us and I won't go easy on you, Zara. I'm a demanding ass when I want to be, both in and out of the bedroom. You should know exactly what you are signing up for before you tell me yes," he said.

Zara's giggle filled his office, "You're so sure I will tell you yes, aren't you Aiden?" she asked. He couldn't help his smile.

"Yes, Zara. I'm used to getting my way and I love a challenge," he said.

"Good to know," she said. Zara stood to leave his office and he suddenly felt flustered. He worried if he let her walk out of there, she might disappear or worse, disappoint him by saying no.

"Where are you going?" he asked. He stood, crossing

the room behind her and stopped dead when she turned to face him.

"I'm going to pick up your daughters from school and then we have a date at the playground. I'm assuming we will see you for dinner?" she asked, cocking an eyebrow at him as if daring him to tell her no.

"Yes," he agreed. "I'll be home by six."

"Good. After I put the girls to bed, I will give you my answer." Zara kissed his cheek and turned to leave without any further fanfare and Aiden wondered just how much control she'd be willing to give up for him. His new nanny seemed to be as bossy as she was capable and Aiden worried he had just bitten off more than he could chew.

ZARA

Zara spent the rest of the afternoon playing with the girls and watching them take endless turns down the sliding board. Honestly, she spent most of her time at the playground trying to figure out just how to answer Aiden's question. Would she really be able to give him what he wanted? She wanted to tell him yes, that she would be his sub and obey his every command in his bedroom but wouldn't that be selling out? She knew she'd eventually want more than just sex—she would want it all, but Aiden was adamant he couldn't give her what she had been dreaming of. Right now, she was concentrating on earning her degree but after she graduated, Zara planned on having some semblance of a normal dating life. He wasn't offering to be her boyfriend and take her out to dinner or to a movie. He wasn't asking to date her—he wanted to fuck her and she needed to decide if that was going to be enough for her.

It wasn't as if she had guys beating down her door offering her anything better but she never thought she'd be someone's sub. Hell, up until a couple of weeks ago, she had no idea what a sub even was. Ava daring her to go to that BDSM club was an eye opening experience for her and she knew once she saw inside that world, she wouldn't want anything less. She was intrigued to learn more and to be honest, experience more. Aiden could give that to her, but she was going to have to let go of her silly schoolgirl ideology of a knight riding in on a white horse with an armful of roses, asking her if she'd go to the dance with him. Aiden wasn't that man and he might never be for her.

After the girls were good and tired, she decided to take them home and give them an early bath. Zara cooked dinner and was just about to give up on Aiden joining them when he came racing through the front door.

"Sorry I'm late, ladies," he said, sounding a little out of breath. "I had a last minute meeting that couldn't wait until morning."

"Do you have to go out again, Daddy?" Lucy questioned. Zara didn't miss the sadness in the little girl's voice.

"Nope," Aiden said. Lucy's face lit up with excitement and she got down from her chair and went over to where the craft supplies were stored. "Good, cause I need help with a card for Rose. It's her birthday soon."

"Right, thanks for the reminder, Lucy. You really keep me on my game. How do you remember Rose's birthday better than I do?" Aiden asked. He pulled Lucy onto his lap and tickled her, making her squirm and giggle.

"Rose says it's cause she doesn't put it on your calendar and you're lost without her," Lucy mock whispered making Aiden chuckle.

"Well, she's not wrong about that, baby. I am lost without Rose. So, I'm guessing she told you it's her birthday soon?" he questioned.

"Nope. She told Zara and I was spying on them," Lucy admitted. She loved to spy on adults, even though Zara had caught her and told her it wasn't nice to listen to other people's conversations. "Rose came over to check on us while you were on your trip. I heard her tell Zara she is going to have a big birthday soon. Can I go to her party?"

Aiden shot Zara a sexy smirk that nearly had her girl parts feel like they might burst. "I'm not sure Rose is going to want a party, Lucy," he said.

"But she said it's a big birthday. I always have birthday parties." Lucy pouted, crossing her arms over her tiny body.

"Rose isn't as excited about her special day as you are for your birthday. It's different for adults," Aiden said.

"How about we bake her some cupcakes and take them by the office? I'm pretty sure her birthday isn't for a few more months, Lucy." Zara interrupted.

Aiden nodded, "See, that sounds like a great idea."

Lucy looked at Laney who sat quietly eating her pasta and they both nodded their agreement. "Fine,"

Lucy said. "But can we get cupcakes tomorrow too? A few months is a really long time to wait." Zara couldn't help her giggle. Lucy was a tough negotiator and she was sure to always be a handful.

"Well, that will be up to Zara," Aiden said. "And, I'm sure it will also depend on both of your behavior."

"I can be good," Laney finally piped up.

"Me too," Lucy promised.

"Well then, I think we can stop at the bakery for a treat," Zara agreed. The girls cheered and celebrated.

"How about you two eat your dinner and then we can play a game before bedtime?" Aiden asked. "If you'd like to play with us, you are welcome to. Or, you can take some down time." Aiden watched her and she thought about taking him up on his offer of some free time. A bubble bath sounded like heaven but the pleading looks on the girls' faces had her changing her mind.

"I'd love to play a game," Zara fibbed. The girls both cheered again and went to work eating their dinner. Aiden went into the kitchen to make himself a plate and then joined them at the table again.

"This looks great," he said.

"It's nothing really. I like to cook and try new things. I didn't have much time to make anything special tonight since we spent a little extra time at the park." Zara wasn't sure why she suddenly felt so nervous around him but she did. She could hear it in her own voice and she worried Aiden would be able to pick up on her sudden case of the jitters. He looked across the table at her and smiled.

"Well, I appreciate you making us all dinner. The girls and I usually do takeout, so this is quite a treat," he admitted. Zara smiled and shyly nodded at him, not quite sure how to react. She was used to making dinner for the kids she worked for, it was part of her services she provided. Plus the families she worked for usually had top of the line kitchens and it was a dream to cook in them.

They finished their dinner listening to Lucy tell the same two stories over and over and Laney even chimed in a few times, when it got to the part where she pushed Lucy on the swings. They were two of the cutest kids Zara had ever seen and she knew getting attached to the families she nannied for was a huge mistake, but there was just something about Lucy and Laney that immediately drew her in—even before she knew Aiden was their father. Maybe it was the little signs of vulnerability Laney showed or the way Lucy overcompensated for her mother's loss by seeking attention. Zara could see herself in both of the girls and it made her want to be there for them, help them in anyway she could. Most of the foster families she was with showed her the same kindness and she knew being a nanny was her way of giving back.

"So, what did you do today, Zara?" Aiden asked, drawing her back to the here and now. He smiled at her and gave a knowing wink. He knew damn well what she did today. First, she packed up her stuff, all the while dreaming about their night together and moved everything to his house and then she had a meeting with him to discuss becoming his sub. All things she could not say in front of the girls.

"Um, well," she stammered. Aiden chuckled and she groused at him. "I got my stuff all moved into my room. I think I'm going to like sleeping in there—night after night," she sassed. There, she could give as good as he could and it was about time she showed him that. Aiden stopped mid chuckle and shot her a displeasing look, telling her that she hit her mark.

"Well, I'm sure you will be very comfortable no matter where you sleep," he said.

"Zara can sleep with me," Lucy piped up. "My bed is super comfortable," she added for good measure.

"Me too," Laney added. "Sleep in my bed, Z," she said, calling Zara by the nickname she had given her. It was what Ava called her too and that thought made her miss her best friend. It was one of the things holding her back from outright accepting Aiden's offer. She knew keeping her relationship a secret from the one person in the world she trusted the most wasn't going to be easy. Ava would demand answers and Zara knew her best friend well enough to know she'd have plenty of questions.

"Thank you both for the kind offers to share your beds but I'm afraid I can't accept," she said to a chorus of both girls groans of displeasure. "You see," she continued, "I snore something awful and I'd just keep the two of you up all night."

"Daddy snores too," Lucy offered. "Sometimes, at night, I hear him and he sounds like a bear," she said.

Laney growled and snarled, causing them all to laugh at the girl's theatrics.

"Now come on girls, you're making Daddy look bad in front of your new nanny. How about we change the subject?" Zara loved that idea. Thinking too much about which bed she wanted to end up in wasn't something she wanted to do. Especially not now in front of both of the girls.

"You both look like you've already had baths," Aiden said. He stood and started clearing the table. "How about I give Zara a hand with the clean up and you two pick out a game to play. And, no Monopoly—I want to get to bed sometime this century." Lucy agreed to pick a game that wouldn't take all night to play and helped Laney down from her chair. Lucy was used to doing so much for herself and Zara didn't want to stifle her independence, but she wished Lucy would learn to lean on her a little more. She had only been there a week and knew it would take some time for both of the girls to fully trust her but she was hopeful it wouldn't take too long.

Zara carried her dish into the kitchen and grabbed the rag to dry the dishes Aiden had started washing. "I wash and you dry?" he asked. She nodded, hoping he'd wait to ask her what she knew he was dying to ask. Honestly, she hadn't made up her mind about his offer yet and she was hoping playing a game might give her some more time to think things through.

"So really, how was the rest of your day?" Aiden asked, handing her another plate. She could tell he was a little nervous and she found the whole domestic scene endearing. The least she could do was meet him halfway, since he was trying so hard.

"After I left your office, I picked up the girls and we spent the afternoon at the park. They sure do love the playground," she said.

Aiden laughed, "Yep. I usually have to bribe them with ice cream to get them to leave."

"Yeah well, we had ice cream cones on the way home," she admitted. "Negotiating with Lucy is like trying to talk down a terrorist. She knows exactly how to get what she wants and goes to great lengths to make things happen. She even got Laney in on her scheme to make me stop for ice cream."

"Lucy can be ruthless when it comes to snacks," he said.

"When we got home, I made them take their baths since they were covered in dirt and chocolate ice cream. I sat in the bathroom with them while they played in the bubble bath and signed up for my last college class I need to graduate. I will need Tuesday and Thursday mornings off this fall, but Rose said that shouldn't be a problem when she hired me. I hope that is still true." Zara waited him out, worried that might be a deal breaker for Aiden. She could see how busy he was with his company and the campaign. Having her take off twice a week, for a few hours might not suit him.

"No, it's fine. Of course your education should come first. You take the time you need and I'll take the girls to school on those mornings. I promise to give you study time too," he said.

"I won't need to take too much time away from the

girls," she admitted. "I will try to get ahead on my Sunday off."

Aiden shrugged, "Whatever works for you, Zara. What happens after you graduate?" She really hadn't given that much thought. Her plan was to get a job teaching and move on with life but telling him that seemed harsh. She knew she couldn't just leave him high and dry. Walking away from the girls might hurt them more than she planned, knowing how their mother so easily left them.

"I haven't given that much thought," she admitted. "I promise to work things out with you and do what's best for Lucy and Laney though. I won't just leave, if that is what you are worried about," she said.

"I appreciate that, Zara," Aiden said. He handed her the last dish and when his fingers brushed hers, she looked up at him to find him watching her. His piercing blue eyes seemed to look right through her and she couldn't help her shiver. "Tell me you've thought about my offer," he demanded.

Zara wanted to lie and say she hadn't really given it much thought but she was sure he'd be able to see right through her. She sighed and nodded, "I have," she admitted.

"And," Aiden asked. He wasn't going to give her a pass on this. He was going to demand an answer and she wasn't sure she had one to give yet.

"It's all I've been able to think about, Aiden," she said. "I just don't—"

"Daddy, we want to play Candy Land," Lucy shouted, running into the kitchen to find them. Zara realized she was standing so close to Aiden she could feel his breath on her face. She took a step back, not wanting to confuse the girls, and handed the dried plate back to him. Aiden looked as frustrated as she felt and she shot him an apologetic smile.

"We will pick this up later," he promised gifting her with his sexy smirk. Zara wasn't sure if she was looking forward to his promise or if she wanted to run and hide away until he forgot he made her the offer in the first place. Becoming his sub was something she wanted more and more with each passing minute, but she also knew wanting something wasn't always a good enough reason to dive into the deep end. Zara was worried she was going to need to learn to sink or swim because Aiden was going to demand his answer and the time was ticking away quickly.

Zara watched as Aiden read to the girls not just one but four bedtime stories until he told them they had enough and tucked them into their beds. She knew both girls usually ended up in one or the other's bed together and Lucy would be up about fourteen times, asking for water and saying she had to use the bathroom; all the while just checking to make sure someone was still there. It broke her heart knowing Lucy felt the need to check to make sure she hadn't been abandoned. Zara wished she could take that uncertainty away from the little girl, but she knew only time could do that. All she could do was show Lucy patience and that she wasn't going anywhere.

She thought about hiding away in her room, but she knew Aiden would search for her and sooner or later she'd have to face him. Zara sat in the family room after putting away all the girls' toys and getting their school bags ready for the next day. When she worked for other families, this was the time she would either go home or to her own room to unwind for the day. But nothing was normal working for Aiden. The fact that she had already slept with her boss was a major difference from her past employment history. She had a feeling working for Aiden was going to be anything but normal and she wasn't sure how she felt about that.

"Hey," he whispered, finding her in the family room. "I thought you might have headed to bed. Sorry, Lucy put up quite the fight tonight," he said.

"I heard," she admitted. "You got out after only four books. That's pretty good. Last night, I had to read six to them before she gave up the fight." Aiden chuckled and sat down next to her on the big sectional sofa. His thigh touched hers and she could feel those same damn sparks like she had every time he touched her body. She wondered if he felt them too but that wasn't something she was ready to ask him. He wrapped his arm around her shoulder and she leaned into him, almost on instinct.

"Zara," he whispered. She squinched her eyes closed and took a deep breath. She knew he was going to ask for her answer and she was no closer to having one to give to him. "Please look at me," he asked.

"I can't," she admitted.

"Why not?" he asked. Aiden rubbed his thumb over her bare shoulder and she shivered.

"Because if I open my eyes and look at you I'm going to see that same hope I saw earlier. You want for me to tell you yes and I'm afraid if I do, it won't be enough," she admitted.

"What won't be enough?" he asked. She could feel his breath on her face, his lips were mere inches from hers and she wanted to open her eyes but knew better.

"Any of it," she said. "I don't want to be a secret, but I know why you can't tell the world about your wife."

"Ex-wife," he amended.

"Right," she said, her eyes still tightly closed. "Listen, I know I was just some woman you picked up at the club and well, things didn't end well. That doesn't mean we should end up together, Aiden. Maybe we should just leave well enough alone and move forward—me as your daughters' nanny and you as my employer."

"What if that's not enough for me, Zara?" Aiden whispered. She couldn't help herself, she peeped one eye open and found just what she expected. He was so close; she didn't dare move for fear of accidently touching him again. If she did, she knew she would agree to just about anything he wanted.

"What do you want, Aiden?" she questioned.

"You," he admitted. He inched closer to her, his lips brushed against hers and she couldn't help but let him take everything he wanted from her. She snaked her arms around his shoulders as he deepened the kiss, sliding his tongue into her mouth to find hers. It was an all consuming kiss and Zara wasn't sure where Aiden ended and she began. He kissed her that night at the club but this was something different, something new and raw. Aiden broke their kiss, leaving them both breathless.

"Wow," she whispered.

"Fucking right, wow," he agreed. "You make me crazy, Zara," he admitted.

"Sorry," she said. "I don't mean to."

"No, it's not something you can control. It's just who you are. Since that night in the club, I've been miserable. I've been beating myself up over how we left things. God, I was an ass and all I could think about was the fact I'd never get another chance with you. I'd never get to tell you that you are all I can think about and I haven't been able to be with any other woman since our night together. But then, you show up here in my bathtub and it's like fate is giving me another chance with you. Please, don't deny me another chance to make things right, Zara. Let me show you how good things can be between the two of us. Let me make up for being an ass and not taking care of you. Your first time should have been so much more than I gave you. Give me a chance to make it up to you. Don't tell me no—not yet. Give me tonight to prove to you I can be enough and if I don't, then tell me no tomorrow."

Zara knew telling him no wasn't something she could do, not now. Not when he was offering her everything she ever dreamed of. She didn't want to hope but she couldn't help it. Aiden was saying all the right things and her brain couldn't sort it all out. Her body was in overdrive from just one scorching kiss and she found herself nodding her agreement before she knew what she was doing. Aiden didn't seem to need any other reassurances from her. He stood and lifted her into his arms, making his way back to his bedroom.

He laid her across his bed. "Be sure, Zara," he commanded.

"I'm sure, Aiden," she said, holding out her arms for him. He covered her body with his own and nothing had ever felt so right as being with Aiden. She felt it the first night they were together at the club and tonight was no different.

"Don't move," he commanded. Aiden took his time kissing her, working his way down her body, taking off her clothes as he went. Once he had her fully naked he stood over her, looking at her. Zara wanted to cover herself and Aiden seemed to be able to tell. "Don't," he warned.

She smiled up at him, "It's like you can read my mind," she teased.

"No, but your expressions give you away, baby. I can see every one of your insecurities looking back at me and there is no reason for any of them. You are so fucking beautiful, Zara," he whispered.

"A girl could get used to hearing those words," she sassed.

"All a girl has to do is agree to be mine and she'll never doubt the validity of those words. I'll prove to you every day just how gorgeous you are, Zara," he promised. "Do you want to play?" he asked.

She wasn't quite sure how to answer him. "Play?" she questioned.

"Yes," he breathed. "Like the night at the club," he said. "Will you give me control over your body tonight?"

Zara nodded, not needing time to think about his request. She loved the way Aiden took care of her at the club and she couldn't wait to see what he had in store for her tonight.

"Good," he said. "Now, get on your knees like a good little girl," he commanded. She hesitated and Aiden waited her out, watching her to see if she'd follow his command. When Zara didn't make a move, he pulled out the big guns, already knowing one of her major weaknesses from their one night together. "I dare you," he amended. Zara felt her breath hitch at his taunt.

"That's not playing fair, Aiden," she pouted.

"No one said I was going to play fair, baby," he said. "What's it going to be, Zara? Are you going to accept my dare and do as I ordered or does this all end here and now?" She thought about getting up and walking out of his bedroom but she remembered how it felt to walk away from him at the club. It hurt and she had to admit, she spent more than one night awake and restless dreaming of being in his bed again. No, she wouldn't walk away again. This time, Zara would accept his challenge because she wasn't going to take the chance of losing him again. She wanted to be daring and take whatever he had planned for her, even if that meant getting on her knees for him.

She slid to the end of the bed and sankdown to her knees in front of Aiden, looking up at him through her lashes. Aiden ran his hand down her face and smiled. "Good girl," he praised and her crazy heart did a flip-flop in her chest. What was it about this man that made her into a giddy schoolgirl every time he told her she had pleased him? She wasn't sure what that was all about but she didn't care. Zara would do whatever it took to hear Aiden call her his "good girl" all night long.

AIDEN

Aiden watched as Zara decided if she wanted to obey his command or not and he knew he was holding his damn breath. She had that effect on him though and his tightly held control would do him no good if he lost his shit and tried to push Zara into something she wasn't ready for. She had the strongest will of any woman he had ever met but their one night together had proven to him she was a natural submissive. She did exactly as he asked of her that night in the club and he hoped she would give him her submission tonight. Hell, if he was being honest, he wanted her submission every night for the foreseeable future but he wouldn't admit that to her for fear of scaring her off.

When Zara sunk to her fucking knees he nearly did the same. He felt himself exhale and when she looked up at him through her long lashes and her tongue softly licked her bottom lip, he couldn't help the moan that escaped his chest. She was his walking wet dream and having her gift him with her submission was everything he could have ever wanted and so much more.

"You are so fucking perfect, baby," Aiden growled his praise and she smiled up at him. His heart felt as if it might beat out of his damn chest and he wasn't sure what to ask for first. He wanted everything from her and all the possibilities played through his mind at once, making it hard to form his next sentence.

Zara waited for his next order and he needed to make a decision. He didn't want to fuck things up with her, but everything he had learned at the club in the last half a year felt like a jumbled mess of information in his head.

"Did I do something wrong?" Zara stuttered. She looked up at him and he could see her uncertainty. That was the last thing he wanted.

"No, baby," he whispered. "You are just so fucking beautiful I needed a minute to get my head together." She gifted him with her shy, sexy smile again and he wasted no time. Aiden stripped out of his clothes, loving the way Zara watched his every move as if she couldn't seem to get enough of his body. When he tugged free from his shirt, Zara's hands darted up to his torso and to his bicep where her fingers traced the outline of his only tattoo.

She softly giggled, "Well, I didn't have you pegged as a shark lover," she teased.

He smiled down at her and shrugged. "That was a very bad decision and a long story," he admitted. "Let's just say I learned not to get drunk with Corbin and let him pick my tattoo." The sound of Zara's laughter filled the room and it was magical. He couldn't remember the last time he felt so at ease with a woman. Towards the end of his marriage to Allison, everything about their relationship felt forced and wrong. He saw that now that things were officially over and they were legally divorced. She couldn't give him what he needed and that wasn't anyone's fault. The only thing he could really fault Allison over was she didn't see the girls often. She'd show up for special occasions, but other than that her visits were few and far between.

"Hey, were did you just go?" Zara asked.

"Sorry," he said. "I was just thinking about how easy it is to be with you." Zara's smile faded and he worried he was admitting too much, too quickly. "No, sorry—just forget I said anything," he covered.

"It's alright, Aiden. I feel the same way about being with you. I know we don't know each other—well, at all but I feel like we do. If that makes any sense," she said. Zara looked down at the floor and he hated he was making her feel so unsure of herself again. He crooked his finger under her chin and lifted her face to look up at him.

"It does make sense, Zara. Thank you for that," he praised. "Are you ready to play?" he hopefully asked.

"Yes," she whispered.

"Good," he said. He knew she had little to no experience; their one night together had proven that fact. He needed to take things slowly but he didn't want to hold back with her. "You need to tell me what you like and don't like, baby," he said. "We are just getting to know each other and I don't want to push you too far. If you don't like something, just tell me to stop and I will." Zara nodded up at him.

This next part was going to be a little tricky, but he needed to ask her questions to get a feel of what to do with her next. "Have you ever given anyone a blow job before, honey?" he asked. She looked down at the floor again and shook her head.

"Eyes on me, baby," he prompted. Zara did as he asked, looking back up at him.

"You must think I'm a complete freak," she admitted. "Honestly, I just concentrated on work and college. I've dated but that was about it." God, she was apologizing for not having any experience with another man and he found that to be the sexiest fucking thing he had ever heard. She didn't realized what a gift she was giving him but he was about to clue her in.

"There is nothing for you to fucking apologize for, Zara. You not being with any other men is hot as fuck. You are letting me be your first for everything and I can't tell you what that does to me. Look at me," he commanded, palming his own cock. He was hard and ready for her attention. He stroked his dick and she couldn't seem to take her eyes off him. "Look at what you do to me, baby," he demanded. Zara licked her lips and moaned.

"Can I," she hesitated, "May I touch you?" she asked.

"Yes," he hissed. "I want you to touch me and taste me," he admitted. The thought of having her lips wrapped around his cock made him even harder, if that was possible. Zara wrapped her small hands around his shaft, taking his directions and pumping his cock. She leaned forward and tentatively licked the head of his dick, gently sucking him into her mouth. It took every ounce of his control not to take over and pump into her hot mouth. He wanted to give her time to adjust to him and explore what he liked and didn't like.

"That's it, baby," he hissed. "Just like that." Aiden wrapped his hands into her long blonde hair and thrust a little deeper into her mouth. She didn't seem to mind when he pushed her a little further, sliding to the back of her throat. When she swallowed around his dick, he nearly came down her throat. Aiden pulled free from her swollen lips and she mewled out her protest.

"I know, baby but if I let you keep doing that to me, this will be over way too quickly," he said.

She smiled up at him, "So, I did it right?" she eagerly asked.

"You were perfect, baby," he praised. "I want inside of you though," he admitted. "Get up on the bed, Zara."

"Will you tie me up again?" she questioned.

"Did you like that, Zara?" he asked.

"Yes," she whispered. "I feel crazy for saying it but I did. I liked everything you did to me that night at the club."

"Good to know, honey. How about tonight we try something a little different?" Zara's enthusiastic nod made him chuckle. "Stand and hold onto the footboard," he ordered. He had a four poster bed in his room and the thought of Zara being handcuffed to the post made him crazy with lust. He watched as she did as he commanded and wrapped her hands around the post, waiting for him to tell her what to do next.

"Perfect, baby," he whispered and slapped her ass. "I'm going to get the handcuffs and then I want to take you from behind," he said. Zara shyly nodded and flexed her fingers on the wooden post, telling him she was just as turned on by his suggestion as he was.

Aiden grabbed the fur-lined handcuffs from his nightstand and secured her wrists around the post. He stood behind her and ran his hand down her back to her curvy backside, cupping her ass in his hands. She moaned and thrusted back into his hold, seeming to need more.

"Are you ready for me, baby?" he questioned. He didn't wait for her to respond, running his fingers down the seam of her ass and into her slick folds. Aiden moaned at finding her more than wet and ready for him. "Mmm, you're ready for me, aren't you baby?"

"Yes Aiden, please," she begged. He lined the head of his cock up to her wet folds and Zara instinctively pushed back against him, allowing the head of his shaft to slide into her slick opening.

"Fuck, baby," he hissed. She was so tight, she nearly milked him. He needed to remember this was all new to her but she felt too good to hold back. He wanted her, all of her and he planned on taking exactly what he needed.

"This is going to be fast, I'm sorry," he said. He pumped in and out of her body, taking what he needed from her and when he knew he was close, he snaked his hand around her body and stroked her clit until she was grinding against him, screaming out his name. Aiden wasn't sure why hearing her shout his name felt so satisfying but it was. He followed her over, finding his own release and pulled her against his body, loving the way she seemed to melt into his hold.

"That was—" she breathlessly stuttered.

"Amazing," he finished for her. Aiden unlocked the handcuffs and pulled her into his arms, depositing her onto the bed. "Wait here, honey," he whispered into her ear, gently kissing her cheek. Zara closed her eyes and hummed incoherently. Aiden went into his bathroom to get a wet washcloth and climbed back into his bed and Zara cuddled into him.

"I'm going to clean you up, honey," he whispered. She opened her eyes and looked at him as if he lost his mind.

"What?" she asked, suspiciously eyeing the washcloth.

"I'm going to take care of you, baby. If you agree to be my sub, this will be part of my responsibilities with you. It will be my job to give you after care and make sure you are alright. Like this," he said. He tried to spread her legs but Zara seemed to want nothing to do with his idea of after care.

"No," she protested. "I can take care of that myself," she insisted.

"Zara," he warned. "Do I need to go over what punishments are and why you might need them or are you going to let me do my job?" Aiden waited her out.

"Fine," she spat. Zara hesitantly spread her legs and covered her eyes with her hands, as if trying to hide. Aiden didn't hide his amused chuckle and when he finished washing her, he pulled her back against his body so she was facing him.

"Look at me, Zara," he commanded. She sighed against his skin and peeped one eye open. "Both eyes, baby," he said. She finally did what he asked, although he could tell she wasn't happy about having to face him. "I'm done playing games, baby. I need to know what you want—I need your answer," he whispered.

Zara smiled at him and his whole world seemed to spin a little faster. "I'll have to follow your every order—you know if I agree to be your sub?" she questioned. He wondered if she was actually considering his offer or if she was just toying with him. Either way, Zara had his full attention. She snuggled into his body, wiggling her sexy little ass against his hands and he flexed his fingers into her fleshy cheeks. He was going to love controlling her every need and desire if she agreed to be his. Aiden was also going to enjoy doling out her punishments and spanking her curvy ass red when she gave him sass, like she currently was. Zara knew exactly what she was doing to him and he had a feeling she'd be trouble at every turn.

"Yep," he said. "After the girls go to bed, you become mine and I like complete control over what is mine," he growled. Zara gasped when he gave her wiggling ass a sharp slap. "Hold still, baby," he ordered. A part of him was surprised when she stopped moving about, proving his original point she was a natural submissive.

"You like it when I spank you, don't you baby?" he questioned. Zara didn't hesitate this time, nodding her agreement.

"I like it when you do just about anything to me, Aiden," she breathlessly admitted.

"So," he coaxed. "Does that mean you will agree to be my sub?"

Again, she showed no sign of hesitation. "Yes," she said. "I will be your sub, Aiden. But we need ground rules if this is going to work out."

He cocked an eyebrow at her and smirked, "What kind of ground rules?" he questioned.

"Well, for one, we can't let the girls know we are—you know sleeping together. No kissing, touching, hugging or any of that type of stuff around them. I know they are your daughters, but I don't want them confused about what is happening between us. Explaining to them what's going on between the two of us might prove difficult since I really have no clue as to what we are doing here," she admitted.

"Well, I think we are two consenting adults having some wicked hot sex, if that helps in way of explanation," he teased. Zara slapped at him and giggled.

"No, Aiden," she chided. He could seriously get used to her stern nanny tone, it turned him on. "This thing between us would be confusing to two little girls. They've been through so much, they don't need to worry about what their father is doing with their nanny," she said.

"Deal," he agreed. "And thank you for caring enough about my daughters to instill such a rule," he said. "It means a lot to me."

"Of course," she said. "I told you I've come to care for

your girls and that wasn't a lie. They are two very special little girls."

"Any other rules?" he asked.

Zara wrinkled her nose and nodded, "Yes—sorry," she admitted.

"How about we sit down tomorrow and go over these ground rules of yours?" he asked.

"That works for me," she agreed.

Aiden wondered how he had gotten so lucky with Rose finding Zara. She really was the perfect nanny for his girls and now, she was going to be his. "Remind me to give Rose a raise," he said. "It couldn't have been easy to find the perfect woman," he whispered.

"Hmm," Zara hummed. "You keep saying things like that to me and I might agree to just about anything you'd like, Mr. Bentley," she said. Aiden didn't want to push his luck but having Zara in his bed was already like a dream come true. He wasn't sure if he deserved asking her for anything else at this point but he wasn't done with her—not by a long shot.

"Well then Miss Joy, you should settle in and get ready for a very long night because I'm about to sing your praises and before you know it you will be my love slave," he teased.

"Deal," she promised. "I'm yours for the rest of the night then." Aiden wanted to remind her she had agreed to be his for every night after this one since agreeing to be his sub but he didn't want to push. Taking things one night at a time was the best for both of them even if his heart did stutter at the idea of having Zara Joy in his bed for good.

ZARA

Zara woke early the next morning and snuck back to her bed before the sun even came up. She managed to get a couple more hours sleep in before her alarm went off. The girls were early risers and she had to get them breakfast and off to school. Plus, the idea of either of the girls wandering into Aiden's room to find them in bed together didn't sit well with her. It would be breaking rule number one and she couldn't have that happen. Her and Aiden's relationship—or whatever it was they were doing together—couldn't touch the girls. Lucy and Laney deserved to be blissfully ignorant of their nanny being their dad's sub.

She brushed her teeth and pulled her hair back, pulling on her robe to pad out to the kitchen to make coffee. Zara wondered if Aiden drank coffee and realized there was so much she didn't know about him. She made a full pot, betting a man with so much on his plate would need some form of caffeine. Although, judging by the way his body looked as if he constantly worked out and took excellent care of himself, maybe he didn't need coffee.

"Morning," he whispered and kissed her cheek. He was already showered and dressed for the day and Zara wondered if Aiden ever got any down time.

"Hey," she whispered back. "You're up early."

"I've been up since you left my bed," he said. "So, I grabbed a shower and decided to get an early start."

Zara smiled and shook her head. "Do you drink coffee?" she questioned.

He looked at her as if she lost her mind. "That is quite a change of topic," he teased.

"I was just thinking I don't really know much about you. You know—likes and dislikes, that sort of thing," she whispered.

He pulled her against his body and a part of her wanted to protest with the girls about to be awake at any moment, but he looked at her as if he wouldn't allow her to raise a fuss about what he was about to do. Aiden pulled her up his body and kissed his way into her mouth, igniting all the same fires that burned during the night when he took her over and over. When he finally broke the kiss, she felt hot and completely out of breath.

"Yes," he said. "I like coffee." Aiden stepped away from her and made his way across the kitchen to pour them both a mug of coffee and all Zara seemed capable of was staring at him with her mouth open.

"Do you have a busy day today?" he asked, handing her a mug.

"Not really. Just running a few errands while the

girls are in pre-school and then they have dance class today." She had only been working for Aiden for a little over a week now, but had found herself fitting right into the girls' schedules. As far as family schedules went, theirs was easy for her to handle and Zara counted herself lucky.

"Will you have time for lunch?" he asked. Zara noticed Aiden seemed a little shy suddenly and she wondered what that was all about. He was usually so in control—so dominant. Seeing him a little unsure of himself did strange things to her heart and she wasn't sure why.

"Lunch?" she questioned.

"Yes," he breathed. "It's the meal between breakfast and dinner," he teased.

Zara quietly giggled and rolled her eyes at him. "Yeah, I have a firm grasp of what lunch is, Aiden. I'm just wondering why you're asking me if I will have time to eat lunch today." It was Aiden's turn to roll his eyes and he set his mug of coffee down and pulled her back into his arms. Zara could easily get used to being held by him, but she didn't want to get her hopes up this was going to be the norm. She needed to remember her own ground rules and once the girls were awake he wouldn't be able to so freely touch her.

"Well," he said, kissing down the column of her neck. "I was thinking you could come to my office and we can order lunch in—just the two of us." Zara wasn't sure what to make of his offer. Wouldn't that be breaking some of the rules? He was supposed to be keeping up the appearance he was happily married for his campaign.

"What if someone sees me?" she questioned. "What about your campaign?"

"No one will see you, Zara," he promised. "Rose is like the crypt keeper when it comes to letting people in and out of my office. She holds the keys tightly and protects me from any unwanted guests."

"She is very protective of you, Aiden," Zara agreed. "But don't you worry about her knowing about us?" she questioned.

Aiden shrugged, "She already knows about us," he admitted. "Well, she knows I met a woman and that woman has been all I can think about these past few weeks. I'm sure Rose is smart enough to put two and two together," he said.

"I was all you could think about—really?" she questioned. Her heart felt about ready to race out of her chest at the way he talked about her. For a man who claimed to only want a sub to play with, he was sure pouring on the romance a bit thick. Zara knew she could be setting her heart up to be broken but she didn't care. Hearing Aiden admit she was all he could think about made her want things she wasn't sure could even exist for them.

"Yes," he whispered, nuzzling her neck. "It seems I still have that problem—not being able to think about anything but you," he admitted.

"Aiden," she murmured.

"Say you'll have lunch with me, Zara," he asked. "Please."

"Yes," she agreed. "I'd love to have lunch with you. I have an hour between errands and picking up the girls. It will have to be an early lunch though," she said.

"Deal," he said, kissing his way up her jaw and taking her lips in a scorching kiss that had her throwing all her rules out the window.

"Daddy," Laney said, standing in the corner of the kitchen, wiping sleep from her eyes. Aiden quickly released Zara and took a step back from her. She knew she was being silly, but Aiden pulling away from her felt like a punishment; as if she had done something wrong. It was crazy, really. She was the one who insisted they have ground rules and the very first one was the girls could not know of their arrangement. They were going to have to be more vigilant in the PDA around the house if they were going to stick with the rules.

"Hey, peanut," Aiden said, crossing the kitchen to scoop up the two year old. "How did you sleep?" he asked.

"Good," Laney said around a yawn. "Lucy's in my bed and she snores." Aiden chuckled and tickled Laney's belly causing her to giggle.

"How about some breakfast?" he asked. "I think Zara's making us pancakes this morning." Laney immediately seemed to perk up at the mention of pancakes.

"Chocolate chips too?" she asked, looking over to where Zara was throwing together the ingredients for breakfast.

"Yep, Squirt," she agreed. "You girls do love your pancakes."

"Well, they get that from me," Aiden admitted. "They are my favorite breakfast food."

Zara smiled, "Well, that's the second thing I've learned about you this morning."

"Second, what was the first?" he asked.

"You like coffee," she reminded him.

"Oh, yes. But I think you learned a little more than just two things about me since you've been here, Zara," he teased, winking at her across the kitchen as if she needed the not so subtle hint he was kidding.

She rolled her eyes and got back to stirring the batter for the pancakes. "Can you wake Lucy?" she asked. Laney squirmed in his arms, trying to get down.

"I can do it," she said. Aiden put the rambunctious toddler down and watched as she ran back upstairs to wake her sister.

"You know she likes to torment Lucy to wake her up, right?" Zara asked.

"Yeah, but I think Lucy gets her back during the day. She is a little bossy towards Laney," Aiden said.

"A little is an understatement," Zara agreed. "Do you think she saw us together?" She knew she was worrying over something that was probably nothing but she couldn't help it.

"No," Aiden said. "And if she did, she's too little to understand what she saw. Lucy is another story. If she caught us, we'd never hear the end of her questions."

"We need to be more careful," Zara whispered.

"How about we discuss all of your rules over our lunch today?" he asked. Zara nodded. She wasn't sure what other rules they should have but she had time to come up with a few. She told Aiden the girls not finding out was her number one rule, but if she was being honest her first rule was to make sure that her heart knew the score. She was his sub and she needed to remember that was all he was offering her. Getting carried away and falling for Aiden Bentley wasn't an option and she needed to remember that rule or she'd walk away from him with one very broken heart.

Zara spent the morning running around town, trying to make sure she got her list of errands finished before having to meet with Aiden. She wasn't sure what to make of his request to have lunch at his office but she was hoping it was more of a date and less business. Zara didn't date her employers, ever. Finding the fine line not to cross between business and pleasure was proving to be tricky. Aiden had seen to her every need and given her plenty of pleasure the night before, but today they would be in his office and anyone might see them together. That thought scared her but not enough to cancel their lunch plans.

She showed up a few minutes early and Rose greeted her at the elevator again. "Hi, Zara," she said. Zara smiled and nodded, not sure how she was supposed to react. Rose had always been gracious and welcoming, but that was before she possibly knew Zara was the woman from the club Aiden had met.

"Hey, Rose," she said. Zara looked to Aiden's closed door and worried he had forgotten about their lunch date—if that was what this was. "Um, is he in?" she asked, nodding to his office.

"Yep and lunch just arrived," Rose said. "He said for you to go right in." Rose went back to her desk leaving Zara standing in the hallway, worried about going into Aiden's office. She wasn't sure if crossing the line between seeing each other in the privacy of his home and the public space of his office was such a good idea but she was about to find out.

"Who do we have here?" A man the size of a mountain was walking straight towards her and she wanted to jump out of his way. Zara looked around, trying to figure out who the man was talking about. "Please tell me you are here to see me?" he questioned, stopping so close to her, Zara had to take a step back from him to look up at his face.

"I'm, um—I'm here to see Mr. Bentley," she squeaked. "Aiden—he's waiting for me," she stuttered. The man took another step towards her again, completely invading her personal space and smiled down at her.

"You shouldn't waste your time on Aiden," he dramatically whispered. "I'm a whole lot more fun," Corbin wrapped an arm around her waist and winked down at her. Zara tried to slap him away but he was a lot bigger than she was.

"Corbin James, let that poor woman go," Rose demanded.

"Oh Mother, you never let me have any fun," Corbin teased. "Besides, I was just about to make my move," he said.

Zara gasped and he had the nerve to laugh. "Get your fucking hands off of my woman." Zara looked around the big man to find Aiden standing just behind him and the expression on his face was murderous.

"Your woman?" Corbin and Rose said in unison. God, Zara wanted to hide but there was no where for her to go. Besides, the big guy still had his arm around her waist and she knew there was no use in struggling.

"Yes, this is Zara," Aiden said. He wasn't really introducing them. It was more like he was issuing a warning and the big guy seemed to take the hint.

"Fuck, Aiden. Why didn't you warn me? When a woman walks in our office looking like Zara here, you know what my first reaction is. A little heads-up would have been nice." He reached a hand out between them for Zara to shake. "I'm Corbin Eklund. Aiden's best friend and business partner," he said. Zara placed her hand in his and he had the nerve to kiss the back of it.

"Zara," she squeaked. She looked him up and down, noticing he was just as handsome as Aiden, about the same age but Corbin had more of an edge to him. His persona screamed bad boy and his outrageous attitude seemed to fit the bill. Aiden seemed to notice her perusal of his business partner, judging by the angry growl that escaped him.

"Well, it's nice to finally meet you, Zara. Aiden has droned on and on about you, so it's nice to put a face to the name," Corbin released her hand and took a step away from her, giving her a full view of Aiden. He didn't look very happy and she was starting to rethink being at his office.

"This was a mistake," she said. "I'm sorry. I should just go," she offered. Zara turned to leave and another frustrated growl ripped through Aiden's chest, stopping her in her tracks. Corbin chuckled and Rose cleared her throat, as if in warning.

"How about we give you two some privacy?" Rose asked. "Corbin take me out to lunch," she ordered.

"Sure, Mom," Corbin agreed. "But listen Zara, if things don't work out with the caveman who has obviously taken over my friend; feel free to look me up. I'm in the office right next to this Neandertal." Corbin brushed past Aiden and slapped him on the back. Aiden shot him a look that would have frightened most men but Zara had a feeling Corbin Eklund wasn't like most other men.

"I'll be gone for an hour, Aiden," Rose said. "And for goodness sake, stop growling at poor Zara," she chided. "See you again soon, Zara," Rose said and pulled her in for a quick side hug and then joined Corbin in the elevator. He smiled and waved at her as the doors closed and she was left alone with Aiden. She turned to face him, not knowing what he was going to do or say next but she was done hiding. If Aiden changed his mind about wanting her there, he was going to have to just tell her that himself. It would hurt to hear he had a change of heart about wanting her, but Zara had lived through worse and she'd get through this—but she wouldn't run away scared, she was done with being afraid.

AIDEN

Aiden watched as Zara slowly turned to face him and he hated he had acted so badly. But seeing Corbin with his arms around her made him half crazy. There was no way he'd let another man touch her—not now that she had agreed to be his. Zara wanted ground rules and he was about to give her them and then some.

"Why were you allowing Corbin to hold you?" he asked.

"Allowing?" Zara questioned. "I wasn't allowing any such thing."

"Then why did I just walk out of my office to find my best friend with his arms around you?" Aiden questioned. He wasn't sure why he was so angry, but seeing Zara in another man's arms made his inner caveman roar to life.

"I'm not sure why you are mad at me, Aiden but you have no right to be. I came here, as you requested, for lunch. I have no idea why your friend thought he should touch me and when I tried to get away, he seemed to

AIDEN

think it was a game. He didn't even know who I was until you stepped in and cleared things up." Zara raised a shaky hand to her face and brushed back a strand of hair that had fallen from her ponytail. He was being an ass and seeing how he had shaken her up made him feel every bit as bad as he should.

"I'm sorry," Aiden sighed. "I'm an ass," he admitted.

"Yes, you are," Zara quickly agreed.

He couldn't help his smile. "You know you could lie and tell me I'm not acting like a jealous asshole," he teased. "Just seeing another man touching you set me off, I guess—I don't know." He tried to shrug it off, as if the whole scene wasn't a big deal but it was. He had blown things completely out of proportion and then when he had a chance to make things right, he blew that too. He needed to get his unruly temper under control or this thing between him and Zara would be over before it even had a chance to begin.

"Well, I'm not a liar. Telling you that you weren't acting like a jealous asshole would be lying," she sassed. "I think now would be a good time for us to go over those ground rules, Aiden." He nodded, knowing she was right. They would have to find some way to navigate through his crazy political agenda and her being his girls' nanny. The odds were already against them succeeding, but that didn't make him want to give up. Quite the opposite—he wanted Zara now more than ever.

"Yes," he agreed. "After this." Aiden closed the space between the two of them and pulled Zara into his arms, sealing his mouth over hers. When she hesitated to let him in, he swatted her ass and she gave a surprised gasp that allowed his tongue access to hers. By the time he finished kissing her, she was breathless and needy, a combination he could work with. After their little discussion and lunch, he planned on taking her on his desk. Hell, if he had his way, he'd take Zara on every surface in his office, but there probably wouldn't be time for that with her having to pick up the girls and Rose returning from lunch.

"When you look at me like that, I worry," Zara whispered.

"Worry?" he questioned.

"Yes. I worry that you are going to eat me alive," she admitted.

Aiden smirked and winked, causing her to turn an adorable shade of pink. "Well, that's not such a bad idea, baby," he teased. "Let's go over the rules first and then we can talk about me eating you." Zara shook her head and giggled and Aiden felt himself relax for the first time since they had coffee that morning. She just had that effect on him.

Aiden sat on the sectional that took up the corner of his office and pulled Zara down onto his lap. "Rose picked us up some lunch. I hope deli sandwiches are okay?" he questioned. "I wasn't sure what you'd like," he admitted.

"Sandwiches sound great," she said. "We really don't know each other, do we?" she asked. They didn't but if Zara gave him a chance, he'd make sure to change that.

He wanted to know everything about her but he also knew that would lead to her being more than just his sub. Aiden didn't know if either of them were ready for that. How would he navigate a relationship that had to be hidden from the public eye? He told Zara before he wouldn't keep her as his dirty little secret and he meant it. If they could just keep things quiet until after the primaries were over, he could somehow come clean with the press and introduce Zara as his—but would she want that?

"So," she said around a mouthful of sandwich. "Ground rules."

"Yes," he agreed. "We have rule number one already down—no letting the girls in on our little secret."

"Right and you almost blew that rule right out of the water this morning. We have to be more careful, Aiden," she chided.

"You're right and it was totally my fault," he admitted. "I just can't seem to keep my hands or lips off you," he teased. Zara giggled as he gave her neck little butterfly kisses. She shivered against him and damn if he didn't want to skip to the part where he took her on his fucking desk.

"The rules, Aiden," she reminded.

"Sorry," he said, even though he wasn't. "So, what should rule number two be?" he asked.

"Um, well I guess you touched on rule number two already—we can't be seen together in public," she said. Yeah—he fucking hated rule number two. Aiden wanted to be able to take Zara out and show her off. Hell, he wanted to go to dinner with her and take her to a movie, but even those simple pleasures would instill a media frenzy.

"For now," he amended. "As soon as these primaries are over, I would like to take you out—you know, on a real date," he said.

Zara smiled and nodded. "I'd like that, Aiden," she agreed.

"Let's add an addendum to rule number two," he said. "How about you let me take you to the club?" he asked. "The one we met at has rules in place for anonymity and as you know, I have a private room."

"But what if someone sees us going into that place together?" she challenged.

"We will just have to take extra precautions," he said. "I had Corbin sneak me in the few times I went, to avoid the press. I'm sure we can work something out. We don't have to do anything you don't want to do, Zara," he said. "As my sub, you will have all the say so, all the power. I can ask but you have the right to say no," he added.

"This is all so new to me," she said. "I have very little experience and this whole Dom/sub thing is completely out of my league."

"I know, baby. That's why we are going to take things nice and slow. I thought the club would get us out of my house on occasion. Plus, it will be like research for you. We can watch other couples play and you can tell me what you'd like to try and what you are against experimenting with."

Zara seemed to mull over his words and then slowly nodded her agreement. "I think I'd like that. I definitely liked watching some of the couples when we were there. I already know I liked when you spanked me," she whispered. Her cheeks turned that cute shade of pink again from her admission.

"Judging by how wet you were, after I finished spanking your ass red, I'd say you loved me spanking you, honey," he said. Zara's tongue darted out and licked her bottom lip and he wanted to moan at the memory of Zara sucking his cock to the back of her throat.

"I liked when you let me taste you," she admitted. "I would like to do that again, Aiden."

"Fuck, baby," when you look at me like that I worry," he teased, giving her own words back to her.

"Worry?" she asked, seeming a little confused.

"Yeah, you look like you want to eat me alive," he joked. Zara's laughter filled his office and he decided the rest of the rules could wait. Two was a good even number to stop at and he had plans for her sassy little mouth. "Up, baby," he commanded.

Zara didn't hesitate; she stood and took his extended hand. "I'm going to give you what you asked for and then I'm going to make a meal of you and fuck you over my desk," he said. Aiden sat down in his chair and Zara sunk to her knees without even being told to.

"Is this okay?" she shyly asked.

It's more than fucking okay," he said. "You are so sexy, Zara." She gifted him with her shy smile and unzipped his pants, letting his cock spring free.

"Mmm," Zara moaned. She ran her small hands over the head of his shaft and he thought for sure he was going to lose it right then and there. Zara leaned forward and sucked him into her mouth, taking most of him and Aiden wrapped her long blonde ponytail around his hand, taking her control from her. He worked his dick in and out of Zara's willing mouth, loving the popping and sucking noises she made every time he pulled his cock free from her lips.

"That feels so fucking good, baby," he moaned. "I'm going to come, Zara," he warned. He tried to pull free from her mouth but she wouldn't allow it. She sucked him to the back of her throat and swallowed around his cock and Aiden couldn't stand anymore. He came in hot spurts down her throat and Zara took all of him, even licking his cock clean when he finished.

"You taste good, Aiden," she said breathlessly.

He leaned back into his chair, catching his own breath and trying to remember how to form words. "God, baby," he whispered. "That was incredible." Again, her radiant smile lit up the room when he praised her. She was such a perfect submissive—from the way she took direction to the way she soaked up his praise; he couldn't ask for more. Well, he shouldn't ask her for more but he was a greedy bastard.

"Up on my desk, honey," he ordered. Zara hopped on top of his desk and he helped her out of her leggings and panties, leaving her bare for him, from the waist down to do with as he pleased. "My turn," he insisted, spreading her legs further apart. He sat back down in his chair and was the perfect height to feast on her pussy. She was already wet for him and she tasted so fucking good.

He ran two fingers down through Zara's wet folds

and licked her clit into his mouth. She moaned and just about bucked off his desk. "Hold still, baby or I'll tie you down." Zara moaned again, as if telling him that idea made her hot. His girl was definitely into kink, he just wondered how far she'd let him push her.

Aiden pumped his two fingers in and out of her wet core, hitting her special spot while he licked and sucked her clit. It didn't take long for Zara to find her orgasm and he loved hearing her shout out his name.

He couldn't stop himself, he stood and let his pants drop to the ground. He was hard again and ready to play, anxious to get inside of Zara. "This is going to be hard and fast, baby," he said. "Rose will be back any minute." Zara whimpered and nodded.

Aiden thrust into her wet pussy and he had to stop and give himself a minute to adjust to the sensation of her tight core gripping his cock like a glove. She spasmed around him and he just about lost it. "Touch yourself, Zara," he commanded. She looked up at him and he could see she wanted to tell him no.

"I—I don't know what to do, Aiden," she whispered.

"Give me your hand," he said. She reached up for him and Aiden took her hand and guided it between where their bodies were joined. "Right here," he said, taking her finger and running the pad over her sensitive nub. She moaned and ground her pussy against his cock. "See, you like that, don't you?" he asked.

She shyly nodded and when he removed his hand from hers, she continued to work her clit. He could feel her orgasm growing and Aiden knew she would be finding her release in no time. He wanted to be with her so he pumped harder into her body, setting a punishing pace.

"Aiden," she shouted.

"Come for me, baby," he whispered, leaning over her body and pumping into her a few more times before finding his own release right along with Zara. She was gorgeous to watch and he wasn't sure what the hell he was going to do about his perfect, secret submissive who was stealing his heart every time she entered the same room as him. Aiden was sure of one thing—rule number three was going to be not to lose his fucking heart to his daughters' nanny.

ZARA

Zara was late picking up the girls and when she ran into their preschool claiming to have been stuck in traffic, their teacher gave her a knowing look. Sure, she probably looked as if she just had a handful of orgasms and her just fucked hair and swollen lips didn't help her case, but spending an hour wrapped up in Aiden was well worth the dirty looks.

"Can we still go to the park?" Lucy asked as she buckled them in the car.

"I'm sorry but not today. You both have dance class and then we have to go home to make dinner. Would you two like to be my little chefs and help me cook tonight?" she asked. They both perked up at the mention of helping her in the kitchen despite not being able to play at the park today.

"Will you stay at dance class?" Lucy asked. "Mommy used to watch us dance," she almost whispered.

Zara was taken aback at Lucy's mention of her mother. The two little girls didn't talk about their mom much. In fact, she didn't realize just how little Allison was brought up until Lucy said her name. "Of course I'll stay to watch my two favorite girls dance," Zara said. "I wouldn't want to be anywhere else." Laney smiled and clapped and Lucy nodded, as if she was satisfied. Lucy was the smartest kid she had ever met and she was sure half of what the little girl did was to test Zara. She worried she had failed most of Lucy's inquiries but she was trying her best. She wanted to be there for the girls, especially since their own mother didn't seem interested in them or anything they were doing.

Aiden had mentioned his ex only came around for holidays and special occasions, but she was missing out on two pretty fantastic kids. Sure the day to day routine could become a little boring, but what mother would want to skip out on any part of her kids' lives? Zara tried to remember it wasn't her place to judge Aiden's ex-wife but the more time she spent with him and the girls, the more she seemed to question Allison Bentley's motives.

They pulled up to dance class two minutes after it started and the instructor shot Zara the same dirty look the girls' teacher had as the three of them raced through the door. What was wrong with people today? It was as if the excuse of being caught in traffic wasn't still a viable one.

Zara sat in the corner of the room, watching the girls spin and twirl, waving to them each time they passed by her. Her phone chimed and she was once again on the receiving end of some very dirty looks, this time from the mothers in the class. Zara mouthed the word, "Sorry," and dug her phone from her purse to silence it. She opened the text from Ava and read her best friend's overly dramatic SOS message. It was the code they used when they had a problem that required immediate attention. Ava was prone to use the SOS message due to a shoe emergency and Zara thought about waiting to call her back, but her phone vibrated with another message and she was sure Ava wasn't going to be ignored. She opened the new message to find Ava's face pop up on her phone screen, her expression dire and Zara stifled her giggle.

She decided to call Ava back, knowing that her friend hated being ignored, it would be her best bet if she wanted any kind of peace. Ava was still angry at her for moving into Aiden's, especially after she told Ava who she was working for. She dialed Ava and held the phone to her ear, hoping whatever crisis her friend was having would be a quick fix.

"You can't make calls in the room during class, Miss," the instructor snapped. Lucy looked completely mortified. Zara didn't know the rules and she apologized and stood to go into the hallway. The way Lucy watched her told her she was going to have to do a whole lot of groveling later if she wanted any peace with the little girl.

"Zara," Ava answered.

"Ava, this better be good and no, a shoe emergency is not a real thing," Zara said.

"This has nothing to do with shoes," Ava said. "I just sent you a link. Put me on speaker and go look at it." Zara decided to humor her friend. She was already in deep water with Lucy and would have to probably bribe her with ice cream on the way home. She opened the link and gasped at the pictures that appeared on her phone screen.

"What the fuck?" she whispered.

"Exactly what I was thinking," Ava agreed. "Tell me the article isn't true, Zara. Tell me you aren't a home wrecker," Ava asked.

"No," she breathed. "How can you even ask me that?" Zara quickly scanned the article that followed the scandalous headline, "New Nanny Breaks up Candidate Bentley's Marriage". The article was full of lies about their relationship and said she had everything to do with Allison Bentley leaving both Aiden and her girls. It spewed some bullshit that Aiden was following Zara's request and keeping the girls from their mother.

"I had to ask, babe. I'm so sorry to be the one to tell you all of this," Ava said.

"What do I do now?" Zara asked. She wasn't really asking Ava; more like trying to figure out her next move. "It all makes sense now," she muttered.

"What does?" Ava asked.

"Why the girls' teachers looked at me as if I was the devil incarnate for being just a few minutes late and why all of the dance moms are spying on me through the windows, as if they are trying to read my lips or something." She turned her back on her audience and worried about any of the hateful lies from the article getting back to either of the girls.

"What if the girls find out?" she whispered.

"Where are you now?" Ava asked.

"The girls' dance class," she said. "They are almost finished."

"When they are done, take them straight home. Do you want me to come over?" Ava asked. She wanted to tell her yes, but Zara worried Aiden would find her best friend at his house to be a breach of confidence. Zara needed a friend right now and there was no way she'd want to turn to anyone else.

"Yes," she whispered. "I'll text you the address and you can meet us there. But not a word in front of the girls."

"Of course not," Ava agreed. "I'll meet you there in thirty minutes." Zara ended the call and turned to go back into the classroom, running straight into a solid wall of muscles. She almost had to strain her neck to see who she had bumped into and the smiling, handsome face looking down at her wasn't quite what she expected.

"You," she said, squinting her eyes at Corbin. "Why are you at the girls' dance class? Wait—don't tell me—you've come here to hit on all the hot, single moms who might be desperate enough to fall for your whole caveman routine." Corbin threw back his head and laughed but Zara found nothing about the situation funny.

"Nope, sorry princess, but I'm here to run a little interference for Aiden and to make sure you and his adorable brats get home safely," he said.

"They aren't brats," she corrected.

"Honey, I've known both of them since birth and let me tell you they are two of the best kids I know, but anything that small and whiney is what I consider a brat." Corbin looked her up and down, as if waiting for her to challenge him but she didn't. Honestly, she just wanted to get home and figure out her next move. The whole news article had her head spinning and a glass of wine with her best friend sounded like the start of a great plan.

"I take it you've seen the article then?" she asked.

"Yep," Corbin confirmed.

"And Aiden," she questioned.

"Has seen and read every lie that was printed about the two of you," he said.

"Well, shit," she whispered.

Corbin chuckled again. "Not the same choice words Aiden used but close," he teased. "That's why I'm here. His team thinks if you're seen out and about town with yours truly, it will take some of the validation out of the lies they printed."

"Or, everyone in town will start talking about how I'm a two- timing whore," she offered. Honestly, she wasn't sure what to do. "Aiden sent you?" she questioned.

"Yep," he said. "He told me to tell you it's going to be alright. He said you'd worry and probably give me a little fight but I reminded him I like my women a little feisty," he teased.

"I'm not your woman," she demanded. Corbin shrugged and smiled down at her as if he didn't hear a word she was saying. Of course he had but he just didn't care. Zara trusted Aiden and if he sent the giant caveman to take her and the girls home, she would go with him.

"Here come the girls," he whispered. "We'll take my car and Aiden will send someone for your SUV," he ordered.

"Uncle Corbin," Laney cheered. The toddler ran to him and held up her arms to be picked up. Lucy on the other hand came out of the classroom with her arms crossed over her chest, wearing a scowl that was directed at Zara.

"Hey, sour puss," Corbin teased; only making Lucy angrier, if that was even possible.

"You said you were going to watch our class," she chided Zara.

"I'm sorry Lucy but I had an important call I had to take," Zara said. The little girls anger didn't seem to deflate any with Zara's explanation.

"Cut it out, squirt," Corbin said. "Zara had something important come up and sometimes us adults have to do adulty things." Lucy stared Corbin down and Zara almost wanted to laugh. Most grown women would have a hard time eyeballing a man the size of Corbin Eklund, but the five year old had no trouble giving him the stink eye.

"She broke her promise," Lucy grumbled.

"Well, I guess you're really mad," Corbin said. "It looks like even ice cream won't make your sister feel any better," Corbin said to Laney. The toddler seemed to play along until she heard the words ice cream and started squirming in Corbin's arms.

"I like ice cream," Laney chanted.

"I know you do short stuff but your sister is just too upset to eat ice cream right now. Looks like I wasted a trip over here to take you girls for ice cream for nothing," he teased.

Lucy dropped her arms to her side, her scowl still in place. "Fine, I'll have some ice cream but I'm still mad at you, Zara. You said you would stay and you lied." Lucy turned around, letting her dance bag hit Corbin's leg and started for the door.

"Lucy," Corbin said, stopping her in her tracks. "You come back here and apologize or we forget about the whole ice cream deal."

"No, it's fine, Corbin. She's right—I let her down and didn't keep my promise." Zara faced Lucy and crouched to be eye level with the stubborn little girl. "I'm so sorry, Lucy. Can you please give me another chance?" Lucy seemed to mull over her decision and Zara found the whole thing adorable, although she wouldn't tell Lucy that. She knew the little girl was still trying for upset but Zara could tell she was letting some of her anger go.

"Will you play a game with me tonight and read me two bedtime stories?" Lucy asked, ever the shrewd negotiator.

Zara smiled, "Of course. But doesn't your dad usually read to you when he's home?"

Lucy nodded, "Yes, but I like the way you do the princess voice." Zara giggled. "How about if you can be the princess and Daddy can be the prince?" Lucy hopefully asked. Corbin barked out his laugh and Zara shot him a warning glance. He held up his big hands, almost as if in defense.

"Well, that sounds perfect," Zara said. "It's a deal." She held out her hand to shake on it and Lucy did the same.

"I'm sorry I was mean to you, Zara," Lucy offered. She turned to Corbin and smiled. "We're good," she said. "Can we go for ice cream now?" Zara didn't hide her giggle. Lucy was always on top of her game and that worried her. She seemed to even have the big guy a little tongue tied.

"Fine," he agreed, scooping Laney back up. "Let's hit the road, girls. Your dad will be home soon and I know he's going to want to talk to Zara. How about I take you girls out for ice cream, just the three of us, while they have their chat?" The girls both cheered and agreed to a special date with Corbin. Zara shuddered at the thought of having to have a private conversation with Aiden about the news article. She was sure he was going to tell her whatever was developing between the two of them was now over before it even had a chance to get started.

AIDEN

Aiden sat in four boring as hell meetings with his advisors and all he could think about was getting home to Zara. She must have been beside herself when she found out about the news article. Sending Corbin to take care of her and the girls might not have been his finest decision but it was all he had. As soon as the story broke, his campaign manager called him to tell him the news. He was furious someone could print so many ruthless lies about him but it was his own fault really. Aiden was the one who agreed to lie about he and Allison still being together and now, he was going to have to come clean publicly about his whole messy divorce. He hated this now involved the new woman in his life—Zara. He was developing feelings for her and he wasn't sure how she was going to respond to the breaking story. Hell, he wouldn't blame her for taking off much like his ex-wife had but he hoped she'd agree to stick around.

His campaign manager begged him not to go public

with his divorce but he didn't see any other way. Pictures of him and Zara had leaked and the worst bit was they were taken right in front of his home. Someone had taken picture of him with Zara and the girls leaving earlier that morning. His manager wanted him to, "clear up the confusion," by telling everyone Zara was nothing more than his daughters' nanny. But, when he explained that was just not the case, he was told to lie about his new relationship or forfeit his candidacy. Aiden was sure there had to be some in between place where they could all meet and find common ground. He just didn't want to believe he'd have to give up one or the other. Zara was quickly becoming an important fixture in his life. The campaign was something he had worked so hard for, giving it up now seemed like failing and that was something Aiden didn't like to do. There had to be a way to have it all, he just needed to figure everything out.

He pulled up to his house and spotted the strange car in his driveway. If another reporter had gotten to Zara or his girls, there'd be hell to pay. He stormed into the house to find Corbin playing Candyland with the girls and no sign of Zara.

"Where is she?" he questioned.

"She's in her room with her friend, Ava," Corbin said, bobbing his eyebrows at Aiden. "You didn't tell me your new nanny had a hot best friend," Corbin said.

"That's because I didn't know about this friend," Aiden complained. "Why the hell is she in my house?" he asked.

Corbin shrugged, "Beats me. She was here when we

pulled up and the two of them disappeared up to Zara's room and I've been watching the rugrats." Lucy and Laney were giggling about something or other and Aiden was happy they were distracted. The last thing he wanted was for either of them to be dragged into his drama.

"Can you stick around for a bit?" Aiden asked. "I need to speak with Zara and straighten this whole mess out—if that's even possible," he said.

"Sure, man," Corbin said. "But don't be hard on Zara. She needed someone to talk to and her friend seems to be on the up and up."

Aiden nodded, "I'm assuming this friend is hot and that's also part of why you're defending her?" Aiden questioned.

Corbin shrugged, "Well, yeah. But your girl has been through a hell of a lot in the past couple days. Just go easy on her."

Aiden kissed the girls on his way upstairs telling them to behave for Uncle Corbin, but Lucy looked to be in rare form tonight, so he was betting that might be challenging for her. "We'll probably go out for ice cream," Corbin called after him but he wasn't paying much attention. His only thought was to get to Zara and make sure she was alright.

"Sounds good," Aiden called back over his shoulder. "Don't be too late—it's a school night."

Aiden found Zara's door shut and he wondered if he should knock. Sure, it was his home but Zara was a grown woman entitled to her own privacy. She had also agreed to be his sub which gave him the authority to enter her room when he pleased and right now, he needed to be with her.

Aiden lightly tapped on the door. "Zara, let me in," he demanded. "We need to talk," he said. He winced at his own words, knowing he sounded like a complete dick. He heard her fumbling around her room and then her door slowly opened to reveal one very pissed off woman whom he assumed to be Zara's best friend.

"Hello," he said. "I'm Aiden—" he wasn't able to get out the rest because Zara's sassy friend held up her hand.

"I know exactly who you are, Mr. Bentley. My best friend is in here crying her eyes out because she feels as though she's done something wrong. But, she hasn't. You, on the other hand, have fucked up royally. How could you let the public believe my girl is a home wrecker? You should have had your people on this already dispelling those vicious rumors and restoring her good name," the woman insisted. Aiden decided immediately he liked her and he was happy Zara had someone so fierce in her corner, fighting for her. He wanted to be that for Zara but at this point, he wasn't sure she'd allow that.

Zara stood from where she was sitting on her bed and crossed the room to face Aiden. He could tell she had been crying and it nearly tore his heart in two. "Baby," he whispered reaching for her. Zara took a step towards him and then hesitated.

"Ava's right, Aiden. Why are you letting this happen?" she questioned.

"I was a fool for listening to my campaign manager. I

should have never let the public believe Allison and I are still married. Hell, it's been over a half a year since she left me and we've been divorced for a while now. I shouldn't have let it go on but I did and I can't take that back. What I can do is fix everything. I've scheduled a press conference for first thing tomorrow morning and I'll be announcing my withdrawal from the race. I'll also be explaining that Allison and I are legally divorced and you are not a homewrecker but someone I am seeing and care for very much," he all but whispered the last part.

"Really?" she squeaked.

"Yes, really," he confirmed. "I was wrong to believe I could run my campaign based on a lie. I could stand here and blame everything on my campaign manager but this was my fault. I take full responsibility and I promise to make everything right," he said. Aiden turned to leave, knowing he had said everything he had to. It was clear Zara's friend, Ava, wasn't going to let him pass and he wouldn't push his way into Zara's room or life.

"Wait," she commanded. Zara turned to her friend and whispered something into her ear and all Aiden could do was stand and watch them, holding his breath, hoping she'd give him another chance. After what seemed like a whispered heated debate, Ava nodded and started past him down the hall.

"You fucking hurt her again and you'll have me to answer to, Mr. Bentley," she promised.

"Duly noted," he said and watched Zara's protective friend disappear down the stairs. He wanted to go to

Zara, pull her into his arms and tell her everything was going to be alright but he couldn't make her that promise.

"Please know that if I could change all of this, I would," he said.

"You would want to change everything?" Zara questioned. "Even everything that has happened between the two of us?" He took two steps towards her, closing the space between them and hesitantly reached for her. When she didn't flinch or step away, he took that as his green light to pull her into his arms.

"Never, baby," he whispered. "I'm so fucking lucky you walked into that club. I wouldn't change one thing about us. I just wish this news article would disappear." Aiden's phone chimed and he pulled it from his pocket to read the text from Corbin.

"Apparently, Corbin and your friend—Ava was it?" Aiden asked. Zara nodded. "Well they are taking the girls for some ice cream Corbin promised Lucy." He smiled at the thought of his daughter's negotiating skills. She was quite ruthless.

"I think Corbin has a thing for Avalon," Zara said.

"Corbin has a thing for just about every woman in the female species. Did he put the moves on your friend?" Aiden asked. Corbin flirted with every woman he had ever met. It was just who his best friend was and he came to accept it long ago.

"No," Zara said. "Just the opposite. You know how forward he was with me earlier?" Aiden nodded, remembering how Corbin couldn't seem to keep his hands to himself at the office earlier that day. He walked out and found his friend with his arms wrapped around his woman and Aiden wanted to pound him.

"Yeah, I remember," he dryly admitted.

Zara giggled, "Well, when I introduced Ava he just stood there, speechless. Since I met him, earlier today, he hasn't shut up and then Avalon walked in and boom—Corbin hasn't spoken a coherent sentence to either of us since. I'm thinking he's either broken or smitten but I don't know him well enough to make that call."

Aiden chuckled at the thought of Corbin being tongue-tied. It would be a first, for sure. "I'd pay good money to see Corbin speechless," he admitted. "This is going to be fun to watch. Apparently, the big guy was able to get himself together and ask Ava if she wanted to go for ice cream."

"I'm sure Lucy helped him with that. Your daughter is a force when she wants something. I'm guessing she gets that from you?" Zara asked.

"So I've been told," Aiden agreed. "Listen," he started, needing to get back to the topic at hand. "I will do everything in my power to fix everything for you, baby. I'm so sorry you had to read that trash."

Zara sobbed and it gutted him. Aiden wrapped his arms around her a little tighter and let her cry into his shirt. "The girls' teachers looked at me as if I had done something wrong," she cried.

"Oh baby, you did nothing wrong," he soothed.

"How did someone get those pictures of us this morning?" she questioned.

"I have no idea, but I have my security team working on finding out who took them and where. I've also increased security for us and the girls. You won't be going anywhere without your guard, understand?" he asked.

Zara slowly nodded. "Is that really necessary?"

Aiden sighed, not wanting to admit this next part. He hoped to avoid painting a picture for her of just how crazy his life could be. "Allison left me for good reason," he admitted. "Can we sit down and talk about this?" he asked.

"You don't have to tell me about your ex-wife or your life prior to meeting me, Aiden. That's not part of the deal we have in place. I'm assuming it isn't a sub's place to know all the gory details from her Doms past," Zara said.

"Fuck the deal, Zara. I want you for more than just my sub. God baby, I want you for—everything. But once I tell you why Allison left me, you might want to pack your shit and run too," he admitted. He hated the thought of Zara walking away from him and the girls. He knew it was crazy and he had only known her a few weeks now but he couldn't imagine his life without her in it.

"Fine, we can talk but I don't think you are giving me enough credit, Aiden. I'm not your ex-wife and I'm sure you aren't fully to blame for what happened between the two of you." Zara took his hand and led him down the stairs to the kitchen. She opened the oven and checked what had been baking, smiling back over her shoulder to where he stood.

"I hope you like lasagna. I made a big pan this morning and stuck it in the oven when we got home from dance. Although, I'm pretty sure Corbin is going to ruin the girls' appetites with ice cream, we can still eat." Zara pulled down two plates and found a bowl of salad in the refrigerator. He could tell she was avoiding having their talk but Aiden would give her a few minutes.

"I'm starving, thank you," he said, taking the plate she handed him. "This looks great," he said. He helped Zara with her plate and then into her chair, at the kitchen table.

"Thanks," she said, scooching up to the table.

Aiden sat next to her and took a deep breath. It was now or never and Zara deserved to know the truth. "Allison left me because she couldn't deal with my crazy schedule or the extra crap that comes with me owning a multi-million dollar corporation." Aiden sat back in his chair, impressed with himself he was able to get that out all in one breath.

Zara looked around his house and smiled, "Yes, I'm sure she hated having to live in a big, fancy house. That poor woman must have been beside herself," she teased.

"I'm serious, Zara," he said. She took a bite of her food and he decided he was going to have to dig a little deeper to show her just how crazy his life could be. "We received four death threats before I left for home tonight," he whispered.

Zara stopped eating and dropped her fork onto her plate. "What do you mean by 'we', Aiden?" she asked. Yeah, now she was beginning to catch on.

"I mean us—you and me. Just before I left, my head of security met with me to go over the new detail assignments and he informed me you and I have had four death threats since this new story broke. It's nothing new for me, but I know this must be terrifying for you. Allison hated that part of our lives. It's why we chose a private preschool and why there is so much security around here and the office," he said.

"You must hate it," she whispered. "Living under a microscope and having to constantly worry about your girls."

"Yeah, it's a part of who I am and what I do. It got worse after I agreed to run for the Senate seat. That's about the time Allison had enough and left us," he confessed.

"Wait—you're telling me you have been carrying around the blame for your ex-wife leaving you all this time? Even Connie says her daughter was a fool for walking out on you guys," Zara said.

"Connie?" he questioned. "She told you about my divorce?"

Zara winced, "Yeah, she's kind of an over sharer."

"Remind me to have a talk with my ex-mother-in-law," he said.

Zara reached across the table and took his hand in hers. "She loves you and the girls, Aiden. She feels awful her daughter so carelessly threw away everything and left you three. She worries about you and the girls," Zara said. "Cut her a break. I don't think you realize how many people in your life truly care about you."

Aiden pulled her from her chair and into his lap. "Are you one of those people, Zara?" he asked.

She shyly nodded and wrapped her arms around his neck. "Yes," she admitted. "I am. Is that okay?" she asked.

"It's more than okay—it's fucking amazing," he said. "But you have to know the good and the bad that comes with me and the girls. We have a lot of baggage and I don't want you to get in so deep you can't find your way out, if you need to."

"I'm not looking for a way out, Aiden," she whispered. "Just let me in, let me show you I can handle all of you, even the bad stuff."

Zara was almost too good to be true but he wouldn't take such a gift for granted. "Alright, but you have to tell me if my crazy life gets to be too much," he said, making her promise.

"Now, let's discuss this crappy idea you have about stepping down from your run for the Senate seat," Zara said.

"It's the only way to keep your name out of the mud they continuously try to drag me through," Aiden offered. "If I continue to run, the press will eat you alive and I can't let that happen."

Zara readjusted her body to straddle his lap and softly kissed his lips. "How about you let me worry about myself and you just worry about your campaign?" she asked.

"You have no idea what you are asking," he said. "The press can be ruthless."

"Well, I've worked for some pretty high profile clients. That's why Rose hired me to be your girls' nanny. Plus, Avalon's family was in politics and I'm sure she can give me some pointers. But, you have to let me talk to her. I know I signed a gag order saying I couldn't discuss you or your family with anyone, but that was before this thing between us happened."

Aiden knew she was right. Corbin warned him that keeping her from being able to talk to her best friend was a mistake and he was right. Zara needed an outlet to vent, especially if she was going to be a part of his life and Aiden wanted that more than anything.

"Fine," he agreed. I will have Rose shred the agreement as long as you promise to use discretion in whom you talk to. Avalon might be the only person you can truly trust. You have to assume everyone else is out for a story and they won't hesitate to profit from whatever piece of juicy gossip they can extract from you."

Zara squealed and squirmed around on his lap and his cock sprang to life. He didn't miss her surprised gasp when she realized what she was doing to him. Her sexy smirk was almost his undoing. "You know, the girls will probably talk Corbin and Ava into a trip to the park," he said. "I think we might have a little time on our hands if you want to skip the rest of dinner."

He kissed his way down Zara's jaw and watched as she tugged her shirt over her head. "No bra?" he asked, making a tsking noise. Zara shook her head and palmed her own breasts, as if offering them to him. "That's sexy as fuck, baby," he said.

Aiden didn't want to waste any time, he stood with her legs still wrapped around his waist and made his way over to the family room, laying her across the sectional. He pulled her yoga pants down her body along with her panties, leaving her completely bare to his gaze.

"You are so fucking hot, baby," he praised. Zara gifted him with her shy smile as he quickly stripped out of his suit. He loved the way she watched him, her heated gaze wondering his body. She laid on the sofa, as if waiting for him to tell her what to do, ever the obedient submissive.

"Up," he ordered. She did as he commanded and he sat down on the velvet sofa and pulled her back onto his lap. Zara straddled his cock and when she slid her wet core over his shaft, taking all of him, they both moaned from the pleasure of it all.

"You feel so good, Aiden," she whispered against his lips. He devoured her mouth, not able to think of anything more than making her completely his.

"You too, baby," he said. Aiden grabbed handfuls of her ass, spreading her cheeks over his cock, opening her further. "I'm going to take your ass," he growled. "Would you like that baby?" he asked. Zara whimpered and nodded her agreement. "Good girl. We will start training your ass soon."

The thought of sliding a plug into Zara's tight, virgin hole nearly had him coming. He needed to make sure she was taken care of first. He ran a finger through her slick folds and then back to her ass, gently probing her hole. She hissed out her breath and threw her head back.

"Yes Aiden, more," she begged. She rode his cock with wild abandon. It was as if she couldn't get enough of him and he loved the way she took what she needed from him. "I'm going to come," she shouted. That was all he needed to hear. He found his release with Zara and when she slumped breathlessly onto his chest, his whole world felt completely right for the first time in a very long time.

"Zara," he whispered. "I think—"

"Hey guys, whoa," Corbin had walked through the front door and turned to quickly usher the girls and Ava back out, closing and locking it, despite their protests. Zara squealed and jumped up, grabbing her clothes to cover her body but it was too late. Judging by his friend's goofy lopsided grin, he had seen every inch of his woman. The big oaf had the nerve to keep staring at her. Aiden stood and covered Zara with his own body but that didn't seem to matter to Corbin.

"Can you please get them out of here and give us a minute?" Aiden questioned.

"Don't worry about the girls and Ava—they didn't see a thing. I forgot Laney's bear and she refused to get ice cream without him," Corbin explained.

"Can you just turn around for a minute, man. Just pretend you are a decent human being and turn your back," Aiden insisted. Zara stood behind him and the string of whispered curses had him smiling. Apparently, Corbin heard her too and laughed.

"You forgot a few choice words, honey," Corbin teased. Zara finished pulling on her shirt and stepped around Aiden, walking straight for Corbin. Aiden pulled on his pants and shirt, preparing for the show he was sure his girl was about to give them. Zara was pissed, reminding him of the way she left the club their first night together. He knew from experience his woman was a spit fire when she was angry and judging by the way she poked her sexy little finger into Corbin's broad chest, she was good and pissed.

"I'm not your honey, Corbin Eklund. You need to knock before you just barge into a room or at least tie a bell around your neck to let us know you're entering." Aiden chuckled and she turned to face him, her expression murderous.

"And you—" she spat.

"Hey, wait a minute. I'm innocent here," he defended.

"You are most certainly not innocent here," she charged. "You knew we agreed to keep this thing between us under wraps. You agreed the girls wouldn't find out and then you took off all of my clothes and looked at me with your sexy eyes and now this—" she yelled, flailing her arms wildly about as if they were helping to prove her point.

"You're right," Aiden conceded. "I fucked up and I'm sorry. We'll just sit the girls down and tell them we're a couple."

"We will do no such thing," Zara shouted.

"Listen, guys," Corbin interrupted. "I'm just going to grab Barry the bear and be on my way." He found Laney's teddy bear sitting on the bench by the front door and gave a wave over his shoulder on his way back out the door. Aiden wasn't sure if he was happy or worried about being alone with Zara again.

"We can't just announce to those little girls I'm your sub and that their Daddy likes to tie their new nanny to his bed," she said. Zara's anger seemed to dissipate some and he had to admit he was glad. She was so much easier to talk to when she wasn't screaming at him and waving her hands around like a crazy person. But, she was right, he fucked up—again. He needed to get his head on straight, but there was something about her that made him want to throw caution out the window and live in the moment. Fucking her on the sofa might not have been his finest decision but it sure felt right at the time.

"Well, we wouldn't tell them any of that, baby. First —I thought we covered the part where you are more than just my sub," he said. "You admitted you care for me and I told you I feel the same way. We might have a Dom/sub relationship in the bedroom but this 'thing', as you keep calling it, has evolved into so much more than that for me." Aiden hoped he wasn't saying too much or pushing her too quickly but he wouldn't hide the truth from her. He was falling for her and it wasn't something he planned on doing—it just happened and it felt right.

Aiden reached for Zara and was thankful she let him pull her into his body. "We'll just tell the girls I'm falling in love with their nanny," he whispered.

ZARA

Zara wasn't sure if she had heard Aiden correctly of if it was her heart interfering with her hearing. "Did you just say you're falling in love with me?" she asked.

"I did," he admitted, without hesitation. "Is it too soon?" he asked. She wanted to tell him it was too fucking fast to be talking about feelings and love. It had only been a couple of days since he found her soaking in his bathtub. But they had their night in the club and if she was being honest, she couldn't stop thinking about him these past few weeks either. There was something about Aiden that had drawn her to him that night in the club and it kept her coming back for more. When he asked her to be his sub she wanted to ask for so much more from him, but she was too afraid of him telling her no. Now, he was offering her his world, his heart and everything she had ever dreamed of and she wasn't sure what to say next.

"Tell me I'm not alone in the way I'm feeling, Zara," he begged. "For fuck's sake, say something," he ordered.

Zara wasn't sure if she was being foolish by admitting it but she didn't care anymore. "You're not alone," she admitted. "I feel the same way but I was too afraid to tell you. I wanted so much more than to just be your sub but I didn't know how to ask," she whispered.

"Thank you for saying that, baby." Aiden wrapped his arms around her and she felt like her whole world was right again. The entire day had been chaotic except for the parts when she was with Aiden. There was something about him that just made her feel as if she was finally home.

"So, we have to tell the girls then?" she asked.

Aiden chuckled, "Yeah, I don't think we have a way around that," he said. "I'm pretty sure I won't be able to keep my hands off you and they are both smart enough to figure this all out for themselves. We need to tell them before someone else does." Zara knew Aiden was right but she worried about upsetting the girls. It hadn't been very long since their mother left and she worried telling them she and Aiden were together might just confuse them. On the other hand, if they heard the news from the whispered rumors that were sure to be circulating about her and Aiden, that would be far worse.

"Fine," she said. "We can tell them when they get home from having ice cream. I promised I'd read Lucy two bedtime stories."

"And how did you get roped into that deal?" Aiden teased.

"I missed watching the last ten minutes of their dance class because Ava called to tell me about the story," she complained. Aiden laughed and she winced. "Yeah, you'll stop laughing when I tell you I promised to do the princess's voice but you have to do the prince's." She was right, Aiden stopped laughing when she told him about his end of the bargain she made with his daughter.

"How did I get sucked into your deal?" he asked.

"Well, it is only fair since the news article was about both of us and it's the main reason I missed watching the end of the dance class." Aiden's pout was adorable and reminded her so much of Laney. Zara took his hand and led him back to the kitchen. "How about I warm our dinners and we can eat before the kids get home?"

Aiden sat down in his chair and pulled her down for a quick kiss. "Deal," he said and then released her. "After we tell them our news, we'll read them their stories and tuck them in, and then I get you all to myself again," he said. She nodded and grabbed his plate. "I think I'd like to tie my little sub up and do all kinds of naughty things tonight," he said. Zara could hear every dirty promise Aiden was making in his gravelly voice and she honestly couldn't wait.

Corbin and Ava didn't get back home with the girls until it was almost their bedtime. Little Laney looked about ready to drop and she wanted to tell Aiden they could talk to the girls another time. Judging by the determined look on his face, he wasn't about to agree to that.

When Zara asked if they had a good time, Corbin mumbled something about them not having as good a time as she and Aiden and Ava looked about ready to punch him. She loved her best friend for wanting to stick up for her, but she had a feeling Ava's reaction had more to do with liking Corbin and less to do with wanting to protect Zara. Aiden was right, it was going to be fun to watch the two of them dance around each other. She had a sneaky feeling it wouldn't take time for them to fall into bed together and a part of her felt bad for Corbin. Avalon was a force and she knew from experience once her friend set her mind to something, there was no stopping her. From the way Ava was staring down Corbin, she more than wanted him and he wasn't going to even know what hit him.

They said their goodnights and Aiden took the girls up for a quick bath while she finished cleaning up the kitchen. By the time she got upstairs, both girls were sitting in Lucy's bed anxiously waiting with their favorite princess books in hand.

"Before we read your stories to you, Zara and I have something we need to talk to you about," Aiden said. Lucy stared him down as if she was ready to negotiate the terms of how long she was going to have to wait for her story. Laney sat back, sucking her thumb, ever the patient one of the two.

"Is this about you and Zara kissing?" Lucy asked.

"Kissing?" Aiden questioned. "When did you see us kissing?"

"This morning," Lucy admitted. "I came down for breakfast and you were kissing in the kitchen," she said, squinching up her nose as if she found the whole idea of kissing utterly disgusting.

"Um, okay—yes. This has to do with Zara and I kissing," Aiden said. He looked over to where she stood in the doorway and motioned for her to get in there and give him a hand. Honestly, she had no idea what to tell the girls. This could completely change her relationship with both of them and she hated that was even a possibility.

Zara sat down on Lucy's bed and pushed back a strand of her wet hair. "Why didn't you say something this morning when you saw your dad and me kissing in the kitchen?" Zara asked.

Lucy shrugged and Zara wasn't sure if she was going to give her an answer or not. "Daddy used to kiss Mommy like that and then she left. I don't want you to leave now." Zara pulled Lucy onto her lap.

"Oh Lucy, I'm not going to leave. Your Daddy kissing your Mommy had nothing to do with why she left. Just because he kissed me doesn't mean I'm going to leave either," Zara said.

"Then why did Mommy leave?" Lucy asked. Zara looked back to Aiden, hoping he'd field that question. She didn't even know Allison, so answering why she left shouldn't be up to her.

"Mommy and Daddy just couldn't stay married anymore, honey. Remember we talked about that when we were on vacation? Mommy decided she needed to live somewhere else and she comes to see you girls when she can." Laney nodded her little head as if she understood every word, but Zara wasn't so sure that was the case. How could someone so small understand such a big problem.

"I remember," Lucy said. "Is Zara going to be our new Mommy?"

Aiden smiled over at her and for just a minute, Zara was sure her entire world had stopped spinning. They were nowhere near that point in their relationship. Hell, as of just two days ago, she was agreeing to be his sub and now he was smiling at her like a loon at the mention of her being the girls' new Mommy.

"No, honey," Aiden said. "Daddy and Zara are dating. Do you know what that means?" he asked.

"Yes," Lucy said excitedly. "I have a boyfriend at school and he said I'm his date." Zara stifled her giggle and it was a good thing, judging from the murderous expression on Aiden's face.

"Well, we can talk about you dating and having a boyfriend when you are much older. The rule is you have to be sixteen before you can date, young lady," Aiden chided. "So you tell this boyfriend of yours you aren't allowed to be his date." Zara cleared her throat, hoping Aiden would take the hint he had gone off course with their little talk. This was supposed to be them explaining to the girls they were together and not him grounding his five year old for seeing a boy behind his back.

"Right," he said. "Do either of you have any questions about Zara and me?"

"I have one," Lucy said, raising her hand as if she was in school. "Will you do the wizard's voice too? Zara should only do girl voices, since she's a girl."

Aiden looked at Zara and smiled, "Yep, I think they are just fine with everything," he said. "And yes, Lucy. I would be happy to do all boy voices, if that makes my little princess happy." Aiden sat forward and tickled both girls until they were giggling uncontrollably.

"Okay, girls. Let's get these bedtime stories done because Daddy is ready for bed." He winked at Zara and she could feel her cheeks heat. Honestly, she was counting down the minutes until she could have Aiden all to herself again, especially with the way he was looking at her like she was his next meal.

AIDEN

Aiden shut off Lucy's light and took one last glance back at his two sleeping daughters. He couldn't believe he was so worried about telling them about him and Zara. They took the news in stride and Lucy didn't seem to miss a beat. His girls were so strong and resilient, he should have known they would be fine with this latest change in their lives.

The house was so quiet, he thought maybe Zara had fallen asleep, but when he walked into his bedroom to find her kneeling in the middle of the floor, completely naked and waiting for him, he felt like the luckiest man on the planet.

"You are so fucking gorgeous, baby," he growled, circling her body. He let his fingers lightly brush her skin and loved the way she shivered with anticipation. "You disappeared after story time," he whispered.

"I wanted to give you and the girls some alone time, in case they had questions they wanted to ask. I worried they might be too shy to ask certain questions in front of me. I'm still so new to them," Zara admitted. Aiden knew Zara cared for his daughters, but hearing just how much made him appreciate her even more.

She looked up at him and paused. "I hope that's okay," she said.

"It's more than okay, honey," he agreed. "I'm just trying to figure out how we got so lucky in finding you," he said. "And now—here you are in my room, kneeling and ready for me—I'm the luckiest fucker on earth."

She gifted him with her shy smile, "Well, you did say I was still your sub and I've done a little research and I think this is right." Zara assumed the kneeling position and put her hands on her thighs, probably having seem pictures of other subs on the internet.

"Baby, you don't have to kneel for me but I have to admit I like it. Seeing you here like this makes me crazy," Aiden whispered. "Come here, Zara," he ordered. He reached a hand down and she didn't hesitate taking it, allowing him to help her up from the floor. Aiden pressed her against his body and kissed her mouth as if he hadn't just taken her hours earlier in his family room. He couldn't get enough of her and he had a feeling he never would.

"I have a surprise for you, honey," he whispered into her ear, loving the way she shivered against him.

"A surprise?" she asked.

"Yep," he almost boasted. Aiden dug into his nightstand drawer and pulled out a blue velvet drawstring bag. "This is for you," he said, handing her the present he ordered for her. Zara hesitantly took the bag and smiled up at him.

"What is it?" she questioned.

"Well, you have to open it to find out," he teased. Honestly, he was a little nervous about giving her something so daring but she did say she wanted to try anal. Zara pulled the little strings and opened the bag letting the three heavy, silver, bullet-shaped butt plugs slide into her dainty hands and looked up at him, questions clouding her beautiful features.

"My question stands. What is it?" she asked. Aiden chuckled and took the anal plugs from her, turning them over in his hand.

"These, my lovely sub, are butt plugs," he whispered the last part.

Zara's gasp was almost comical but he knew better than to laugh at her right now. This was another new toy he was hoping she'd agree to; so there was no place for humor. "You have all the power here, baby. You say the word and I put these back in the bag and we forget the whole idea," he offered.

Zara squinched up her nose and took the anal plugs back from him. She looked over each one carefully and help up the smallest one. "I wouldn't mind this one," she said, handing it over to him.

"That's my girl," he praised. "And yes, it's always best to start small and go up in size to train your ass." He gently pulled her along to his bed and sat on the edge, patting his thighs. "Over you go," he ordered.

Zara did as he asked, laying over his lap with her ass up and ready for him. "I'm going to spank your ass red and then I'll put this in," he said. "I want you to put it into your mouth and suck on it until I finish spanking you," he ordered. She took the plug and looked at it as if it offended her.

"Like a pacifier?" she questioned.

"Yes," he said. "I've already cleaned it and your saliva will act like a lube, along with your arousal. Plus, your mouth will help warm the metal and that will be a lot more comfortable for you, honey." Zara nodded and took the plug from him and gingerly sucked it into her mouth. Watching her do what he asked always made him hot, but knowing she agreed to letting him train her ass was over the top sexy.

"Fuck, that's hot, honey," he said. She settled on his lap squirming against his cock and he was sorry he had decided to spank her first. He knew she liked to be spanked but he wasn't sure if his cock liked the fact he was going to have to patiently wait his turn.

"I'll count, since your mouth is full," he teased. She squirmed about and he gave her fleshy ass a good swat, knowing the first blow had to sting the most. "One," he whispered, rubbing where he landed the first slap. He alternated cheeks, never landing in the same place twice and worked her up to twenty and stopped. Her pussy was soaked; he could feel just what his spanking did to her every time he'd dip his fingers through her folds and back to her ass.

Aiden knew Zara was fully in the zone when he asked her for the plug and she seemed to ignore him. He gently pulled the metal piece from her mouth and she moaned her protest. "Sorry, honey but I need in that tight little pussy of yours now. We can play some more later." Aiden parted her ass cheeks and ran the warm metal plug through her drenched pussy, gathering her natural lube to help the plug slide into her ass. Zara whimpered and bucked on his lap and he landed another sharp slap to her ass.

"Hold still, Zara," he ordered. "I will tie you up if you can't be a good girl for me," he threatened. From the moan that ripped from her chest, she like the idea of him having to tie her to the bed. He worked the smallest plug into her ass and she seemed to fight it at first.

"Just relax, Zara," he ordered. "This will be so much easier if you don't fight it, baby." Zara took a deep breath and he could feel her whole body relax across his lap. He worked the plug past her tight ring and when he had it fully inserted he inspected his handy work, loving the way the little blue jewel peeked back out at him.

He helped her off his lap and onto the bed. Aiden quickly stripped out of his clothes, loving the way she shamelessly watched him. "Spread your legs for me, honey," he ordered. Zara did and he could see the plug was still firmly inserted into her virgin hole. The thought of being able to take her ass had him nearly coming into his hand. Aiden grabbed her legs and shoved his cock into her pussy with one thrust, causing her to cry out.

He stilled inside of her worried he hurt her. "Tell me you're okay, baby," he said through gritted teeth. It was taking all his willpower not to move.

"I'm good, Aiden," she purred. "I just feel so full with both holes filled," she admitted.

"You feel tighter, honey," he agreed. "This is going to be fast." He pulled his dick free from Zara's drenched folds and slammed back into her, repeating that move over and over until she cried out his name. Aiden pumped into her body a few more times and lost himself deep inside of her and collapsed on the bed next to Zara.

"Well, that was different," she teased. "I think I like my new gift."

"I'm happy to hear that, baby because you have to leave it in all night," he taunted.

"All night?" she asked. "Yep, and I'll be checking in the morning to make sure it's still there. If not, I'll have to come up with another punishment for tomorrow night." Zara groaned and rolled over to cuddle into his side. He chuckled and kissed the top of her head. "Now you're getting it, honey."

ZARA

Zara woke the next morning to Aiden standing over her gently spreading her ass cheeks, to check to see if the plug was still in. "Good girl," he praised and she heaved out her sigh of relief. She hadn't slept much during the night, worried she would relax and let it fall out. She rolled over to face him and Aiden's face turned from amused to worried.

"You look awful, honey. Are you alright?" he asked.

"Gee, thanks for that," she teased and got out of his bed. "I didn't sleep well," she admitted.

"Is my bed uncomfortable?" he asked.

"No," she stretched and yawned, loving the way Aiden's gaze roamed her naked body. "Your butt plug was uncomfortable. Every time I started to let myself fully relax and drift off; I was afraid that damn thing would fall out."

"Fuck," he swore. "I didn't think about that. How about we train your ass during the day, so we don't interrupt your sleep. I'm sorry," he said. He turned her around and bent her over the bed, so her ass was once again presented to him.

"What are you doing?" she squeaked. She had learned not to question Aiden, knowing that nine out of ten times she loved every kinky thing he did to her.

"I'm taking the plug out and you can wear it some tomorrow. Let's give this sexy ass a break," he said. He gave her a smack and pulled the plug free. Her entire core spasmed and she wasn't sure if she felt relief it was out or if she already missed the weight of it filling her.

"Let's get you into the shower," he ordered. "We need to get a move on if I'm going to make my meeting this morning and fire my campaign manager," he said.

"So, you're really going to do it then? Fire her and quit your campaign?" Zara hated the idea of him giving up his dream because of her. She wanted him to be happy and Zara worried quitting his run for the Senate would be a huge mistake.

"I think it's for the best," he whispered. "I won't have you hurt by all of this." Zara turned and wrapped her arms around his neck.

"I'm fine, Aiden. You do what is right for you and I'll find a way to deal with the press and the gossip. No matter what you do today, I'll be alright," she promised. And, she would be. That was who she was and it wasn't going to stop now just because some vicious lies were circulating about her and Aiden.

"How did I get so lucky?" he questioned. "I think I've waited all my life for you, Zara Joy. You are the perfect woman and the perfect submissive." Hearing him say those words did crazy things to her heart. She wanted to tell him she felt the same way but he didn't give her the chance to.

"Come on," he insisted. "We're going to have a shower and then breakfast. I'm sure my munchkins will be up and demanding pancakes before we can get our clothes on." He turned on the shower and cleaned her plug while they waited for the water to heat up.

"What's on your mind, Zara?" he asked.

"Um, nothing really," she squeaked. But, that wasn't the truth. She had questions that were probably none of her business but she still wanted to ask them. Zara knew she might be a little pushy asking him about his ex-wife but she felt as though she needed to know.

"Out with it," he demanded, pulling her into the shower with him. The hot spray felt like heaven and she almost forgot wanting to play twenty questions with Aiden. He cleared his throat, staring her down and Zara knew she wasn't going to get out of asking.

"You said that you and your ex didn't really do the whole Dom/sub thing," she said.

"Right," he confirmed. "Allison wasn't into the whole scene. "Maybe that was why she ended up leaving or maybe I unknowingly pushed her away. Either way, I'm happy with the way things worked out. I would have never met you if she didn't leave me." Aiden soaped up her body with his hands and kissed the column of her neck. She leaned back against his big body, loving the way he took care of her.

"You keep this up and you definitely won't make your meeting," she sassed. He chuckled and thrust her body under the spray, grabbing her shampoo.

"Get your hair wet and turn around," he ordered. He worked the shampoo through her long blonde hair and his fingers felt like magic massaging her scalp.

"Mmm, You're good at this, Aiden." Zara was pretty sure she'd like to start each day this way.

"Rinse," he ordered, turning her into the spray of water again. She rinsed her hair, watching him as he lathered up his own body. Everything about the man was sexy and she wasn't sure if she'd ever get enough of him or his bossy nature.

"Did you ever ask Allison for this?" She gestured between their bodies and Aiden shyly nodded, making her instantly regret her question. He was usually so confident and in control, but now she could see his self doubt.

"I did," he confirmed. "She told me I was a freak." He laughed at what he said, as if he had told Zara a joke. "I believe the term she used was 'sexual deviant'," he said.

Zara reached up to frame his face with her hands. "You are not a sexual deviant, Aiden. You are Dominant and there is nothing wrong with you."

Aiden nodded and smiled. "And you are my beautiful submissive. You're pretty perfect yourself, baby," he said, causing her heart to feel as if it might beat right out of her damn chest again. Zara wasn't sure what they were doing together or where this thing between them was headed but she was ready to find out. Being with Aiden was like having all her dreams fulfilled and she wasn't ready to let that go—not yet at least.

Aiden agreed to talk with the press at his office and Rose set up the conference scheduled for ten in the morning. That gave Zara just enough time to get the girls to school and run over to his building. He told her she didn't have to be there but it didn't feel right not to be.

He had gone in early that morning to meet with his campaign manager. After their meeting, he ominously texted Zara, "It is done" and she wasn't sure if she wanted to cry or giggle. She hated how her being in his life was costing Aiden so much, even if he told her she was wrong every time she brought it up.

Zara texted Rose she was going to come to the conference and Rose told her to come up to Aiden's office using the private elevators for staff to avoid the growing members of the press that had gathered in the building's lobby. Rose met Zara at the elevator as usual and smiled at her.

"He's going to be so happy you made it," Rose said.

"I don't know about that," Zara admitted. "This morning he told me not to worry about coming over but how could I not? This mess is because of me and I feel as if I need to be here for him, even if I'm hiding behind the scenes like a coward."

"The press is watching for you, Zara. It's best you don't give them what they want and stay out of sight. They are like a pack of hungry wolves, but this media frenzy will die down—it always does." Zara wished she could be as positive as Rose, but she had been a bundle of nerves since Aiden left the house this morning.

Rose tapped on Aiden's door and he barked for her

to come in. Zara shot Rose a look, probably something akin to terror and Rose just shook her head and smiled. "Aiden, Zara is here to see you," Rose shouted back. She opened the door and let Zara pass into the office. Aiden stood and met her halfway.

"Why are you here, baby? Is everything alright?" He pulled her into his arms, not waiting for her to answer. She sighed against his chest, wrapping her arms around his waist.

"Now it is," she admitted.

"Did the press see you come in? Did they say something to upset you?" he asked.

"No," she said. "Rose had me use the employee entrance and elevator and they don't even know I'm here."

"Good," he said. "I don't want them bothering you and after this conference, I'm pretty sure they'll leave us both alone."

"Aiden, I—" she wasn't sure what to say next. How did she tell him she thought it was a huge mistake giving up his run for the Senate seat? Was it her place to tell him to run? "You shouldn't quit," she whispered.

"We've been over this already," he said. "I won't jeopardize you or the girls to further my political career."

"I appreciate that, I really do. But the girls and I aren't in jeopardy," she said. "You can't let them win like this. If you quit now, you'll be playing right into their hands."

"What do you suggest I do then?" he asked. Aiden released her and paced his spacious office. "I can't let the press hound you at every turn," he growled in frustration.

"You've already increased security and you've fired your campaign manager. Don't make any more hasty decisions until you have time to think things through and hire a new manager." She hoped Aiden saw her point of view. It was getting to be time for the conference and she hated to see him throw everything away.

Rose popped her head into his office, "It's time, Aiden," she said.

He gave a curt nod. "I'll be right there," he said. She left the office again and Aiden pulled Zara against his body and crushed her mouth with his own. When he broke their kiss, she was panting—not sure if it was due to lack of oxygen or desire.

"Will you be here when I get done?" he asked.

"Of course," she whispered. "I'm not going anywhere. I'll be watching on your television."

Aiden smiled and walked out of his office and she wanted to stop him, worried she was letting him go off to make the biggest mistake of his life, but she had already done all she could. The rest was up to Aiden now.

AIDEN

Aiden faced down the noisy mob that had gathered in his office's lobby and for the first time in a long time, he wasn't sure what to do next. He stood at the podium and waited for the unruly crowd to settle and when they were finally quiet, he cleared his throat to begin. He pulled the notes he made from his suit pocket and nodded to the crowd.

"Thank you all for coming today. I wish it was under better circumstances," he admitted. "The other day, a story leaked that my new nanny, Miss Zara Joy and I are engaged in an affair. That news is true." He once again had to wait for the crowd to quiet in order to continue.

"Please, let me finish," he ordered. Aiden looked up the atrium, as if he would possibly be able to see Zara watching him from over one hundred floors up but that would be impossible. Just knowing she was in the same building gave him the courage to continue.

"I wouldn't exactly call it an affair since neither of us

are married," he said. "Allison Bentley and I have been estranged for almost a half a year now. I did not meet Miss Joy until a few weeks ago and she has only been my daughters' nanny for a couple of weeks. I was under the misconception that I needed to keep my divorce a secret or risk ruining my campaign," he admitted. "The person who made that advisement is no longer with my campaign and from this point on, I will tirelessly work to keep an open dialogue with the press. All I ask in return is for you to give my family the courtesy of some privacy. My daughters and Miss Joy are not running for office—I am. I ask that you leave them out of this campaign and I, in return, will have an open door policy with a promise of no more secrets."

Aiden looked around the room and paused. This was the point in his speech when he was going to announce he was dropping out of the race but the words felt like they were stuck in his throat. He wondered if Zara might be right and he might be making the biggest mistake of his life by dropping out of the race. He could at least wait until he found another advisor, as she suggested. A few weeks wouldn't hurt.

"Thank you for your time," he said and turned to go back upstairs to where Zara was waiting for him. Corbin flanked his side, wearing a goofy grin. "Don't," Aiden ordered. The crowd erupted into a frenzy of questions and Aiden ignored them, stepping into the elevator with Corbin. He watched as his security team tried to keep the crowd at bay and he worried he had just made a crucial mistake.

"What have I just done?" he whispered as the elevator doors closed, shutting out the chaos.

"You just took your chance, man. I have to say, I'm pretty fucking proud of you," Corbin said, slapping him on the back.

"Thanks man. I just hope I didn't make things worse," he said. He thought about how the hell he was going to keep the girls and Zara safe and Aiden worried he'd never be able to. He might have taken a chance, but at what cost? Playing with Zara and his daughters' safety wasn't a part of the plan.

A month had passed and Aiden was no closer to finding a new campaign manager. For now, he was winging it but he wasn't sure how much longer that would work. Zara and the girls seemed to be adjusting to life as the family unit they were quickly becoming. They didn't even hide the fact he and Zara were sleeping in the same room anymore. The girls seemed fine with it all and he had to admit that took a huge weight off his shoulders.

Zara was about to start her last class to finish up her degree and they had worked out a nice rhythm that suited all of them. While Zara was in class or studying, he tried to pick up the slack and when he couldn't Rose or Connie helped out. It was nice to feel like part of a team again and it was damn nice to feel like he had a partner in life.

Zara stormed into his office and slammed the door

behind her. She was beautiful when she was angry and she seemed to be pretty damn pissed about something and he was sure her ire was directed at him. Rose opened his office door, popped her head in to mouth "sorry" to him and quickly retreated—being the smart coward she was.

Aiden sat back in his chair and crossed his arms over his chest. Zara looked him over and seemed to lose a little of her anger. "You can't do that," she grouched.

"Do what, baby?" he asked but he knew exactly what he was doing. He usually tried to deflect her foul mood with sex and now was no different.

"You are using your body to try to make me forget how mad I am at you," she shouted.

Aiden chuckled and put his feet up on his desk and she actually growled at him. "This isn't funny, Aiden," she yelled.

"Okay, how about you start out by telling me why you are so angry with me," he asked. Zara threw a piece of paper onto his desk and pointed at it as if it offended her in some way.

"That," she said. Aiden picked it up and looked it over, grimacing when he read the part, "Paid in full." He had found her college bill laying on the kitchen counter a few weeks prior and decided to pay it for her. He knew Zara had struggled to pay her college tuition each semester and her bill was nothing for him. Aiden wasn't one to ever flaunt his money, but he had enough to take care of his family for generations to come. He considered Zara a part of his family now, but he worried pointing all that out might move her from pissed to ready to inflict bodily harm. He needed to tread carefully if he was going to get through this conversation with her and come out unscathed.

"Let me just explain," he said.

"Yes, I would love to hear how you went behind my back and paid my college tuition for the semester," she shouted. "You have no right, Aiden."

"You're right," he agreed. "I went behind your back and paid your bill for the semester. Where you are a little fuzzy is the part where you say I had no right to do it. I had every right, Zara because you are mine and I take care of what's mine." He stood and rounded his desk, slipping in between it and where Zara stood so she was facing him. She wouldn't be able to escape looking at him and that was just fine with him. He needed for her to completely understand how he felt about her. Aiden wasn't a fool—he knew telling Zara he had fallen in love with her would probably send her running for the hills, but he needed her to understand he'd always take care of her. He wanted forever with her, but he'd keep that little piece of information to himself for now.

"You can't just go around throwing money at my problems to make them go away, Aiden. You and I live very different lives." He wrapped his arms around her and pulled Zara against his body.

"No," he disagreed. "You and I are now living the same life. You are mine and if I want to give you a gift, I will. If I want to do something to make your life a little easier—I will and if I want to take care of you, I will. You need to accept the fact that you are a part of my life now, Zara and I am a very rich man. I haven't always been, so I know where you are coming from but I won't hide who I am now."

"But—" she tried to protest but he stole her next words with his kiss. He kissed her until he could feel all the hostility she had worked up against him leave her tightly wound body. Zara relaxed into his arms and he chanced breaking their kiss.

"But nothing, baby. You either want me or you don't," he said, holding his arms wide as if challenging her to tell him she wasn't interested.

Zara sighed and finally gifted him with her shy smile. "I want you," she agreed. "God help me, I want all of you."

Aiden didn't hide his smirk, "Thank fuck, baby. I want all of you too. Can we put this behind us?" he asked.

Zara hesitantly nodded. "Yes, as long as you promise from now on before you do something to help make my life easier, we talk about it first. I don't want to feel blindsided again."

"Of course," Aiden agreed. "Any other stipulations?" he asked.

"No, and thank you," she whispered. "I'd offer to pay you back but I'm pretty sure that will piss you off," Zara said.

"Damn straight it will. And, you're welcome," he said, wrapping her in his arms again. "Now can we get to the part where I distract you with my body?"

Zara giggled, "I have just over an hour before I pick

up the girls from school," she said. "Will that be enough time?" she asked, giving him an exaggerated wink.

Aiden laughed, "Challenge accepted," he agreed and started stripping Zara out of her clothes. He always loved a good challenge and Zara gave him one at every turn.

ZARA

One Month Later

Zara ran into the school hating that she was once again late. The girls' teachers already thought the worst of her and she wasn't helping her case, but her doctor's appointment had run over since the nurse couldn't seem to find her damn vein. They poked her twice before getting blood and then she had to wait in a line to pay her bill but what choice did she have. She had been feeling sick and rundown for weeks now and had put off going to find out what the problem was. Honestly, she had always been a little afraid of needles and doctors and everything that went along with them. Today was just not her day and being ten minutes late to pick up Lucy and Laney was just the icing on the cake. She knew the little negotiators were going to talk her into ice cream and tonight was the big fundraiser for Aiden and their sort of coming out as a couple party to test the waters. Since he hired a new campaign

ZARA

manager a few weeks prior, she felt more at ease attending functions with Aiden. Still, it took some coaxing on his part to convince her to go with him. There would always be haters and if she wanted to be the woman on his arm, Zara was going to have to suck it up and deal with them.

"I'm so sorry I'm late," she said, breathless from her run in from the SUV.

"You're not late," Lucy's teacher said. She had a fake smile plastered on her face and Zara was sure she wasn't going to like whatever the woman planned to say next.

"But I am," she admitted, checking her watch. "I'm ten minutes late. I got stuck at the doctor's but that's no excuse."

"No, you're not late because the girls were already picked up," the teacher said.

"Picked up?" Zara questioned. "By whom?" She knew for a fact Aiden had back-to-back meetings all afternoon and Connie was feeling a bit under the weather.

"Mrs. Bentley came to pick up her daughters," the teacher said. She almost seemed happy about delivering the news to Zara, as if it gave her some perverse pleasure.

"Allison's not supposed to have them. She didn't let Aiden know she was going to get the girls." Every one of Zara's red flags were flapping in the wind and she worried the worst.

"Well, Mrs. Bentley is still the girls' mother and Mr. Bentley hasn't removed her from the list of possible people allowed to pick the girls up. You'll have to talk to him about that, but we had no reason to keep her from her daughters." The teacher looked her up and down as if mentally sizing her up and then turned on her heel to go back to cleaning up the classroom, effectively dismissing her.

Zara pulled her cell from her bag on the way out of the school. She needed to tell Aiden that Allison had the girls. A part of her hoped he knew about it but had forgotten to tell her, but deep down she knew something was wrong.

"Rose," Zara shouted into the phone before Rose had a chance to even get the company name out. "Allison picked the girls up from school today. She took them," Zara choked back her sob with her last statement. She needed to keep her calm or she'd be no good to anyone, especially not the girls.

"What?" Rose questioned. "Hold on, let me grab Aiden," Rose said and put the call on hold.

Within seconds, Aiden was on the other end of the call. "Zara, tell me where you are," he ordered.

"I'm standing outside the girls' school," she said.

"Get in the fucking SUV and stay there. I'm on my way. Allison has kidnapped the girls and I have my team on it," Aiden said.

This time, she didn't hide her sob. "Oh my God, Aiden. How do you know she took them?" she asked. Zara looked around the parking lot as if making sure she wasn't being watched.

"She left a note with her mother. She visited Connie this morning and when she took a nap, Allison was gone. She left a note saying she wouldn't sit back and let me be happy with someone else. It said she wouldn't let the girls be raised by any woman but herself." Aiden's voice cracked and it was nearly her undoing.

"I'm so sorry, Aiden. This is all my fault—I was late picking them up," she sobbed.

"Where the hell were you, Zara?" he growled.

"I wasn't feeling well and ran to the doctor," she admitted. "I'm going to go to your house to see if maybe she's there." It was worth a shot. Allison might have had a change of heart and decide to take them back home.

"No," Aiden barked. "If she's there and you show up, she could be provoked to anger. I don't want her to lose her temper around the girls or you. Get in your car and stay put." Zara could tell he wasn't in the mood to be questioned.

"Fine," she agreed. "But find them, Aiden," she begged.

"I will honey, don't worry about that," he promised and ended the call. Zara didn't care if she was sitting in the middle of the girls' school parking lot or the fact that any reporter could come along and take her picture. She covered her face and this time, she didn't muffle her sob. If she would have just waited to go to the doctor, she wouldn't have been late to pick up the girls and they never would have gone with Allison. She worried they would never see Lucy or Laney again and the thought of Aiden losing his girls tore her heart apart. Zara was sure he'd never forgive her.

She knew if she sat in the parking lot and obeyed Aiden's orders she might be risking losing the girls forever. Zara was closer to the house than Aiden was and with traffic this late in the day, she'd be able to beat him there by almost thirty minutes. That was precious time they might not get back and she knew she had to at least try to look for them.

"I'm sorry, Aiden," she whispered and put the car in drive. Zara was going to go back to the house and hopefully, she'd find Allison and the girls there and she wouldn't let her take them anywhere if she could help it.

Zara pulled into the driveway and parked behind the white car she assumed to be Allison's. "Got you," she whispered. She thought about calling Aiden, but she didn't have time to argue with him about whether or not she should go in. She already knew what his answer would be, so she decided to text him instead.

At the house and her car is here. Going in.

Zara sent the text and turned off her phone and tossed it into her purse, not wanting to take the chance Aiden would call her back to talk her out of going into the house. If the girls were in there, nothing would stop her from getting to them.

The front door was open and Zara stuck her head in, worried she was too late. It was unusually quiet; too quiet for both girls to be home. "Come all the way in—Zara is it?" A tall, thin woman stood in the corner of the family room with her arms crossed over her chest. Zara knew from the pictures Aiden kept in the girls' rooms that she was Allison; though she looked thinner than

ZARA

her pictures portrayed her to be and with the dark circles under her eyes, she didn't look like herself much at all.

"Where are the girls?" Zara asked.

"Do you mean MY girls?" Allison shouted. "My girls are safely tucked away so you and I can have a little chat."

Zara wasn't sure if she was relieved or worried the girls weren't at the house. That meant she and Allison were all alone and Aiden had warned that might not end well for her. "You knew I'd come here looking for them, didn't you?" Zara questioned.

"Yep," Allison said, seeming almost proud of herself. "You are predictable. Poor Aiden. I know he likes things a little spicy and you must completely bore him," Allison taunted. Zara refused to answer, not wanting to give in to the woman's provoking jabs. She didn't owe Aiden's ex-wife any explanation.

"What do you want?" Zara asked.

"Well, that's a simple question. I'll give you a very simple answer. I want for you to leave," Allison spat.

"Why now? You've been gone for almost a year and you and Aiden aren't even married anymore," Zara said. She knew she was poking the bear so to speak, but she couldn't help herself.

"I've heard all about you, Zara. You're disgusting the way you swooped in here to take my husband and girls. The media had you pegged from the beginning—you're a homewrecker, nothing more. Once I realized what you were doing here, I had to step up and save my family. You left me no choice."

"So, this is a selfless act on your part and has nothing to do with the fact that you look like you've been living on the streets and most likely hooked on either drugs or booze," Zara spat. She was done letting everyone think she was a homewrecker. She met Aiden after his divorce was final and she wasn't about to stand there and let Allison spew lies about her. Connie had hinted to her she was afraid her daughter was caught up with the wrong people and possibly hooked on drugs. She said Allison's boyfriend had kicked her out when she ran out of money and she had shown up a few times at Connie's begging for cash.

"How dare you," Allison yelled. "You have no right to judge me. You, along with your self-righteous attitude, can go fuck yourself. I've been through hell since leaving here and I'm ready for my life back. You'll just have to step aside, sweetheart because I'm taking back what's mine and that includes Aiden." Zara barked out her laugh and took a step towards Allison.

"You don't get to come waltzing back in here to demand your life back, Allison. You walked away from the best man I've ever met and your daughters deserved more from their mother. How could you just throw them all away? No, you won't be taking anyone back— it's too late for any of that," Zara said. She turned to leave, knowing she had said everything she needed to. Allison would never concede and they had reached a stalemate. She'd never convince Allison she wasn't right for Aiden and the girls and really, why would she bother?

"Stop," Allison shouted. "Stop or I'll shoot." Zara's

blood ran cold at the sound of the gun cocking and she slowly turned to find Allison holding a handgun that was pointed right at her. "You stupid bitch," Allison yelled. "You are making me do this, aren't you?"

Zara held up her hands, not wanting to give Allison any reason to pull the trigger. "I'm not making you do anything, Allison," she said. "Please just let me go and no one will know I saw you here. No one will know we even had this conversation," she begged.

"I'm supposed to just let you walk out of here and then what?" Allison asked. That was a good question. Zara wouldn't let Allison take the girls—Aiden would never forgive her. But, she needed her to believe she would.

"You let me go and then you can pick up the girls and disappear. I'm sure I can convince Aiden they are better off with you. It will give you a fresh start and I know they miss you," Zara lied.

"They do?" the woman questioned. Zara almost felt bad for lying to her; Allison looked so hopeful when she mentioned the girls.

"Of course they do," she said. "You're their mother."

"That's right, I am," Allison shouted. "And you're trying to take that all away from me. You're just a low-rent whore," she yelled.

Zara could feel her hot tears streaming down her face blurring the world around her. She noticed movement out on the patio and her eyes must have given her away. Allison turned, training her gun on the French doors that led to the outside space. "Who's there?" she yelled. Zara wasn't sure if her eyes were playing tricks on her or not, but she could have sworn she saw Aiden pass by the window and she knew if he barged in on the two of them, it would only piss Allison off further. It was now or never and she had to take her chance. Zara turned and ran towards the open door, knowing if she could make it just a few more steps, she would be clear of Allison's threat and hopefully be able to warn Aiden his ex was armed and dangerous.

The shot rang out and Zara wasn't sure who was shouting—a woman or a man—they both sounded the same. The ringing in her ears was almost as painful as the searing, hot, pain that ran down her thigh and into her left leg. She was falling and there was nothing she could do to stop it, but instead of hitting the ground she looked up to see Aiden's intense blue eyes looking back at her. He had caught her and she was sure he always would.

Zara, baby, stay with me," Aiden ordered. She wanted to tell him she would stay with him for the rest of her life if he'd ask her to, but when she opened her mouth to speak, no words came out. The world around her seem like a dream and the last thing she remembered hearing was a woman's voice screaming Aiden's name. Just before her world faded to black, she realized that woman was her and she was sure she had just looked at the man she loved for the very last time —Aiden.

AIDEN

After Aiden got off the phone with Zara, Connie called him to tell him Allison had doubled back to drop the girls off at her house and said something about finding Zara. She mentioned having to set her straight and Connie worried her daughter was about to do something stupid. She was sure Allison was on something and he knew if given the chance, she'd hurt Zara. He couldn't let that happen. Corbin was with him and they headed for Aiden's house, believing Allison would look for Zara there first.

Zara texted she had found Allison's car in his driveway and he panicked. Aiden knew it was a trap, but he couldn't reach Zara to tell her what was happening. He called in his security team and he and Corbin decided not to wait for back-up. There was no way he'd let Allison hurt Zara—she was his whole world.

Peeking in the patio windows hadn't afforded much insight as to what was going on inside his home, but judging by the way Zara stood with her hands in the air,

Allison had a gun pointed at her. Aiden motioned to Corbin he was going around the house and through the front door and his friend agreed to take care of his ex-wife. He knew Corbin would get some secret personal satisfaction taking Allison down and that was fine with him. All he could think about was getting to Zara and keeping her safe, at any cost. But he was too late. By the time he reached the front door, Aiden found Zara running towards him and just before she got to him, Allison shot her in the thigh. Zara stumbled towards him and fell into his arms screaming his name and he felt completely helpless. She passed out and he removed his belt, making a tourniquet for Zara's leg to help stop the bleeding.

Aiden heard a commotion in the house and from the sounds of Allison's protest, Corbin had secured her and the gun. "You good out there, Aiden?" Corbin shouted. He emerged from the house dragging Allison along with him, her gun in his other hand.

"Fuck," Corbin swore, looking at Zara.

"She shot Zara," Aiden choked. Corbin slipped the gun into the waistband of his pants and pulled his cell phone from his jacket pocket.

"Don't worry man, I'll get help here before you know it. Just keep pressure on the wound," Corbin ordered. Aiden felt as if his world was moving in slow motion as he sat on the ground holding Zara against his body. There was blood everywhere and he worried she had already lost too much.

"Why, Allison?" he shouted. She stood next to Corbin, her arms pinned behind her back by his friend, looking down on him as if he had some nerve asking her why she'd shot Zara.

"You had no right being with her," she answered. "She wasn't good for my daughters or you."

"You don't get to decide that anymore, Allison," he yelled. "You divorced me. You're the one who chose to leave us. Zara came into our lives and took care of the girls. She loved me without questioning who I am or telling me there is something wrong with me for what I liked."

"You're a pervert, Aiden. I wouldn't give in to your disgusting needs so you pushed me away. Maybe you were with her this whole time, who knows. But you stopped wanting me the day I told you I wouldn't play your disgusting kinky games," Allison said. She looked down her nose at him with a self-righteous look on her smug face and he wanted to tell her she was wrong but he wasn't sure he could. Allison and he grew apart towards the end of their marriage and even though he didn't turn to anyone else, as she had, he did push her away.

"You're not right about everything, Allison. In fact you've twisted a few of the facts around. You were the one who cheated in our relationship. What was I supposed to do, look the other way while you dated other men? Our marriage was one of convenience for you, wasn't it Allison? You married me because you were pregnant and then you got too comfortable to leave. My only fault was not seeing it sooner. I let things go on for too long and when you left I was angry at myself because I felt as if I let the girls down. But you know what really ate me up with guilt?" He paused, as if waiting for her to answer but he really didn't care if she did or not.

"I felt relieved you finally left me," he whispered. "I beat myself up over that for so long but now I see I shouldn't have."

Corbin ended his call, "They'll be here in less than five minutes now. I'll meet our security team with Alli here."

Allison thrashed and bucked, trying to get free from his hold and Corbin seemed to be enjoying the fact she couldn't. "Not going to happen, sweetheart," Corbin growled.

"You can't hold me against my will," she complained. "Aiden and I are talking."

"You're done talking, Alli," Corbin said. He turned to Aiden, "Man, she's high and no amount of reasoning will get through to her. She shot the woman you love, Aiden."

Aiden knew Corbin was right. The woman who stood before him now wasn't the same woman who he fell in love with all those years ago. He could see that now. "Take her," he spat. "We're done talking."

"No," She screamed, panicked. "You can't do this, Aiden. She deserved it. She's nothing. You can't love her." Corbin pulled her along down Aiden's driveway, leaving him alone with Zara to wait for the ambulance to get there.

"She's wrong," he whispered to Zara. "I do love you—more than anything. Please be okay, baby."

Aiden felt about ready to go out of his mind. It had been two days of hospitals, doctors, and nurses giving him polite stares and endless worry Zara wasn't going to wake up. He was allowed to ride with her to the hospital on the ambulance, but when they got her into the emergency room, they took her from him and he wasn't allowed to see much of her. A few of the nice nurses bent the rules and let him into Zara's room but he wasn't always so lucky. No one would give him any answers and it was starting to piss him off. All the doctors would tell him was she was doing well, was stable and still hadn't woken up from surgery. They asked if Zara had any family they could call and according to Avalon, she didn't. He knew her parents had died when she was just a girl, but hearing Zara had been completely alone in the world made his heart hurt. She was lucky to have Ava in her life but he wondered just how lucky she'd consider herself to have Aiden as part of it. He was the one who dragged her into his mess. He was the one who asked her to keep their relationship a secret, as if she was someone he was embarrassed of. He was the one who put her in danger, not realizing just how messed up his ex-wife was.

The local authorities had arrested Allison and were holding her without bail, since she was considered a flight risk. They had sent her to a local rehab facility and Aiden hoped she'd get the help she needed. Allison wouldn't be a part of their lives again but he had loved her and she gave him two precious girls. If Lucy and

Laney decided to know their mother when they were older he wouldn't stop them, but he just hoped Allison would be clean for such an occasion. He would never want his girls to see their mother like she was the day she broke into his house and tried to kill Zara. She wasn't the same woman he remembered and he knew the drugs had changed her. He was just not ready for how much of her they had taken; she was just a shell of her former self and that made Aiden sad for her.

Corbin and Rose had been stopping by daily to check on Zara. Corbin had picked up the slack around the office because there was no way Aiden was going to leave Zara, if he could help it. He had made sure the girls got to where they needed to go and had spent just enough time at home to shower and change. Other than that, he had taken up residence in the hospital waiting room and prayed someone would give him some good news.

Corbin strolled into the waiting area with Lucy and Laney. He picked them up earlier from Connie's so Aiden wouldn't have to run across town again. "Daddy," Laney squealed, running to jump into his arms.

"Hey Laney girl. How was school?" he asked.

"Good," she said, nodding her little head.

"How about you, Lucy?" he questioned.

"I got in trouble for telling the new kid there was a rule she had to push me on the swing during free time," she admitted. Corbin laughed and Aiden shot him a look to cut it out.

"We've been over this before, Lucy. You can't force people to play with you and lying isn't something that is allowed in our family," Aiden chided. His daughter dutifully nodded her head, but he could tell she really wasn't paying much attention to him. She was too busy looking around the hospital probably seeing what she could get herself in to.

"My teacher wants to talk to you," she muttered.

Aiden sighed, knowing the routine all too well. His daughter had acted out just like this when Allison left them. Now, with Zara all but disappearing from her life, she was back to her old tricks. Lucy loved to tell other kids what to do—it was a gift. She even would go as far as lying to them to get them to do her bidding. Sure, she was probably an evil genius, but he was getting sick of being called into parent- teacher conferences to discuss his little angel's behavior.

"I will talk to her tomorrow when I drop you off. You will have to be punished for what you did, Lucy. I'll decide that after I talk to your teacher." Lucy looked down at the floor and nodded and he almost wanted to let her slide this time. Aiden knew he couldn't, otherwise she'd be back up to her tricks in no time.

"Any word on Zara?" Corbin asked.

"No, man. It's driving me nuts not knowing what's going on with her," Aiden said.

One of the doctors who usually gave him vague updates on Zara popped his head into the waiting room. "Mr. Bentley, Miss Joy is awake and asking to see you," he said.

"I want to see Zara," Lucy demanded.

"Me too," Laney quickly agreed.

"You two peanuts are going to stay with me," Corbin

said. "Let your dad check on Z and when she's feeling up to it, you can have a visit with her." Aiden nodded his thanks to Corbin and started for the door, anxious to get back to her.

"Thanks, man. I owe you," Aiden said.

"Damn straight you do," Corbin agreed. "This is probably going to cost me another trip for ice cream."

Aiden didn't care what it cost him. Hearing Zara was awake and wanted him was the best thing he had heard in over two days. He'd make sure she was alright and then he was going to convince Zara she needed a family and if he had his way, he'd do everything in his power to make sure his own family fit the bill.

ZARA

Zara felt groggy and her entire body hurt. The nurse said that was normal for someone who had been in a coma for the past two days. The last thing she remembered was Aiden catching her after Allison shot her and judging from the cast on her leg, she hadn't missed. Even small movements sent shooting pains up her leg and when she asked for pain medication, the nurse smiled and nodded, telling her the doctor would have to talk to her about that before she could give her something and she didn't have the energy to argue with her. Honestly, she just wanted to see Aiden to make sure he and the girls were safe. She had so many questions to aske him but they could wait.

"Hey," Aiden stood in her doorway and she wondered how long he had been standing there.

"Hey yourself," she croaked and cleared her throat. Zara wasn't able to hold her sob in and Aiden was immediately by her side. He carefully sat on her bed and gently pulled her against his body.

"You scared the shit out of me," he whispered, kissing her forehead. "I'm so happy you are awake; they wouldn't let me back to see you and I worried—" his voice broke and Zara could hear his pent-up fear. She hated how she made him worry that way.

"I'm so sorry," she murmured against his chest. "This was all my fault. If I had just listened to you and stayed in my car, none of this would have happened. I was just worried you wouldn't have gotten there in time and Allison would take the girls. I couldn't allow that."

"I know, honey. When it comes to loving my girls, you are as fierce as they come. I'm so happy they have you," Aiden admitted.

"I love them, Aiden. I can't imagine my life without Lucy or Laney," she said. Zara wondered if Aiden would want to know she felt the same way about him, because she did. She was just too afraid to tell him she had fallen in love with him. They hadn't said those words to each other and she worried about being the first to come right out with them.

"I know, baby." Aiden seemed to hesitate and she worried she had said too much. "How do you feel about their dad?" he whispered. It was almost as if he could read her mind. She could feel his heart beating and could tell he was just as nervous about this as she was. But not giving him the words; not being completely honest with him felt wrong.

"Um," she squeaked. "I feel the same way about him as I do his girls," she admitted.

"Thank fuck," he exhaled. "When I thought I lost you, Zara—God, my whole world collapsed. I sat in that fucking waiting room for two days, worried I'd never see you again. I worried I'd never be able to tell you I've fallen completely in love with you, baby."

"You have?" she interrupted.

"Yes," he said. "Look at me, baby," he demanded. Zara was afraid to look at him for fear she'd burst into tears but really that ship had already sailed. Since Aiden had walked into her room, she was a sobbing mess. She chanced a look up at him, his blue eyes looking back at her with so much promise and love, she wasn't sure how she had missed it before.

"Hi," he whispered. Aiden leaned in to gently brush her lips with his own and she thought it was the sweetest gesture. "Marry me, Zara," he said.

Zara gasped and covered her mouth with her shaking hand. "Aiden," she sobbed. "You can't mean it."

"I can and I do," he said. "When you stumbled into that club, I thought you were the most beautiful woman I had ever seen. Then, you agreed to be mine and I thought you were the perfect submissive. I was sure I couldn't ask for anything more but I was wrong, Zara. I want more from you. I need for you to be my wife, honey. I want you to be the woman who I come home to every night and the person I wake up next to every morning. Be mine, Zara—marry me."

Zara wasted no time answering his command. She was already his—body, mind and spirit. Agreeing to marry him wasn't something she needed to think about. It was what she had always wanted but never let herself hope for.

"Yes," she breathed. "I'm already yours, Aiden and I'd

love to marry you." Aiden gently kissed her lips and Zara knew in an instant her entire life had changed. She wasn't sure what she had done to deserve the man sitting next to her but she wasn't about to try to figure it out.

"Um, I'm sorry to interrupt." the doctor who had been in earlier after she woke up pushed the door open, letting himself into the room. "How are you feeling, Miss Joy?" he asked.

Zara nodded and winced, "My leg is killing me. Can I get some pain medication? The nurse who was in here earlier told me you would have to approve it." The doctor nodded and looked nervously between her and Aiden.

"Yes," he said. "Um, I'd like to talk to you privately, Miss Joy." Aiden's frustrated growl seemed to startle the poor doctor. She wanted to giggle but knew better than to poke Aiden when he was angry.

"Aiden can stay," she offered.

"Well, I need to go over a few things having to do with your medical history. He's not your family member, so maybe it would be best to discuss everything, just the two of us." The doctor winced as if he was expecting Aiden to fly off the bed and attack.

Zara worried the same thing, placing a hand on Aiden's thigh, trying to calm him. "Aiden has just asked me to marry him, so technically, he's about to be family. You can discuss anything you need to with me and my fiancé."

The doctor nodded and smiled. Aiden seemed to relax a little beside her and Zara wondered if he was always going to be so protective of her. "Is something wrong?" she asked.

"That depends on what your definition of wrong might be," the doctor said. "You're pregnant, Miss Joy." The doctor crossed the small room and pushed a button on a machine that sat by her bed. Suddenly, a swooshing sound filled the room and she looked at Aiden and back to the doctor.

"Is that sound coming from my body?" she asked.

The doctor smiled and nodded again. "Well, technically yes. It's your baby's heartbeat. We've been monitoring everything since your surgery, and he or she has a very strong heartbeat. We estimate you're about two months along," he said.

"That's impossible," she said. "We were careful."

"No contraceptive is one hundred percent effective," the doctor said. "I will order some pain medication that will be safe for you and your baby but it won't fully relieve your pain. I'm sorry." He turned to leave the room and a part of Zara wanted to yell for him to come back. She had a million questions she wanted to ask and the thought of having to face Aiden alone frightened her. He had been so quiet since the doctor announced she was pregnant, she worried he would be angry or worse, disappointed in her news.

"Aiden," she said. Zara wished he would look at her but he seemed distracted by the baby's heartbeat monitor. Aiden stood and walked over to where the machine was measuring the baby's heartbeats per minute and it was as if he didn't even hear her call his name.

"I didn't mean for this to happen," she admitted.

Zara hated thinking Aiden might believe she had trapped him. She knew Allison was pregnant with Lucy when they got married and she would never want him to marry her just because she was pregnant.

"If you've changed your mind about marrying me, I won't blame you," she almost whispered. Aiden turned to face her and she could tell he was angry.

"Why would I change my mind about marrying you?" he questioned. She shrugged, not knowing how to answer him.

"You didn't plan for this," she pointed to the machine and then back to her still flat tummy. "I wouldn't blame you if you wanted to rethink your proposal. Maybe we should just take some time and rethink all of this. I just need time, Aiden. Please, can you do that for me?" Aiden nodded and opened his mouth to say something, closing it again. He turned and walked out of her hospital room without another word. She wanted to get out of that damn bed and chase him down the hallway to tell him she was wrong but that was impossible. She didn't want to push Aiden into something he didn't want and from the way he so easily walked out of her room, the baby wasn't something he wanted.

Zara had taken the pain medication and the doctor once again assured her it was safe for the baby. She already felt a strong protective nature when she thought about the life growing inside of her. Her doctor said it was a miracle she didn't lose the baby with all the stress and trauma of having to deal with being shot and undergoing surgery. They removed the bullet and had to put a metal rod and screws in where it had spliced her bone, but the doctor was confident she would make a full recovery in a few months. Zara wasn't so sure about her broken heart though.

She spent the rest of the day after Aiden left sleeping and even dozed in and out most of the next day. Every time she woke, she would question the nurses if he had been back to see her and their sympathetic looks gave her their answer before they even opened their mouths. Ava had been by to visit her a couple of times and she gave Zara the same look of pity every time she'd ask about Aiden.

"He'll come around, Z," Avalon promised. "He's just dealing with a lot right now—give him time." She wanted to childishly point out she was dealing with a lot too but she didn't. Zara just hoped Ava was right and Aiden would come to accept the baby, even if he didn't want her anymore. Her son or daughter had the right to have him as part of their life but she wouldn't force him to take part. Zara just hated the idea of her baby not having both parents' love. Aiden was a fantastic father. She didn't want her baby to miss out on having him as a dad.

The hospital kept her for two more weeks and when she was released, Zara wasn't sure where she was supposed to go. All her stuff was at Aiden's house but she wasn't going to just show up there. She made arrangements to stay at Ava's and the nurse told her that her health care would cover a visiting nurse for her therapy and recovery. She didn't want to be a burden on anyone. Zara wished she could say she was finding a way to get over the loss of not having Aiden and the girls in her life but she wasn't. Each passing day was harder and harder. She missed them so much, she wasn't sure she would ever be able to move on, but for the sake of her child she was going to have to find a way.

Ava picked her up at the hospital and helped her into her SUV. "I'm so happy to be out of that place," she whispered after getting settled in her seat. "Thanks for doing this, Ava," she said.

"No problem, Z. I just have one quick stop to make and then we'll get you settled," Avalon said. Zara would go anywhere if it meant she didn't have to spend another minute in that hospital.

They started driving and Zara tried to lay back and relax but getting comfortable was nearly impossible. The pain medication had made her a little fuzzy and she must have dozed off because when she woke up, she was sitting in Aiden's driveway. Ava turned off her vehicle and shot her a guilty look.

"Sorry, Z but he made me promise not to spill the beans," she said.

"Spill the beans? What beans?" Zara asked, confused about the whole situation until Aiden stepped from the front door dressed in a tux. Lucy and Laney sprang out from behind him, both dressed in long flowery dresses and she wondered if they were interrupting one of Aiden's fundraisers.

"What the hell is going on here?" Zara questioned.

"Well, you are about to marry that man—right there," Ava explained, pointing to Aiden.

"He walked out on me. He left me to sit in that hospital room for almost two weeks, believing he wasn't ever coming back," Zara sobbed.

"I know, Z. He was a complete asshole and he feels bad. Just let him explain," she said nodding to the passenger side window where Aiden stood. The girls had gone back into the house and Ava got out of her SUV to follow them in, leaving Zara and Aiden completely alone.

She crossed her arms over her chest and looked straight ahead. "You left me and now you expect for me to just marry you?" She said, summarizing what Ava had just explained.

"I know and I'm so sorry," he admitted. "It was a fucked up thing to do and I didn't know how to make it up to you. I was afraid of messing things up with you like I had Allison and when you told me you didn't want to marry me and you needed time, I freaked out."

"So what, I'm supposed to just forgive you and say that I'll marry you?" she questioned.

"Well, that would be nice but judging from your tone, I don't think that is going to happen," he teased. "Please, Zara," he begged. Aiden opened her car door and gently pulled her into his arms, careful of her leg. "Please let me show you we can make this work. I want you and our baby. I want you to be my wife. I knew I wanted more children with you, we're just having the first one sooner rather than later. Say you'll marry me," he begged. "I've arranged everything. All you have to do is say yes and come with me into the backyard."

"You mean now, as in today? You want me to marry you in the backyard, right now?" she questioned.

"Yes," he simply said. "Ava picked a dress out for you and I have everything arranged. Tell me you still want to spend the rest of your life with me," he asked. Zara wasn't sure what the hell to do. But she knew if she told him no, she'd be making the biggest mistake of her life. She wanted Aiden and the girls and telling him no wasn't an option.

"You just left me at the hospital, Aiden. I thought you didn't want me or our baby," she whispered. Zara thought she had lost him for good when he didn't return and it broke her heart. She didn't want to risk losing him again—this time possibly for good.

"I know and I'm so sorry," he said. "Your doctor told me any upset could possibly hurt you and the baby. I couldn't chance losing either of you," he admitted. "Tell me you'll marry me, honey. Let me make it all up to you," he begged.

She nodded and Aiden lifted her into his arms, crushing her against his body. "What are you doing?" she asked. "I have crutches and can walk."

"I know that, baby. I'm just not giving you a chance to change your mind again," he admitted. She wasn't about to tell him that wouldn't happen. She was his, now and forever. Nothing would ever change that for her, even her own stubbornness.

AIDEN

Aiden paced outside the master bedroom, wearing a path in the hallway's floor boards, waiting for Zara to finish dressing. He wasn't taking any chances with letting her get away from him again, even blocking the damn entrance so she couldn't change her mind. Hearing her tell him she needed time just about ripped his damn heart out of his chest but he wanted to give that to her. Aiden wanted her to be sure about marrying him and if he was being honest, he was too stubborn and too hurt to go back to that hospital. He wanted to barge into her room and demand she take him back but he wouldn't chance upsetting her. On his way out of her room, her doctor explained she needed complete calm and rest or she could possibly lose the baby. He received the doctor's message loud and clear and left Zara to get the sleep she needed to recover. But waiting for her one minute past her release from that hospital was damn near impossible for him. He wanted to pick her up from there, but Ava convinced him it would be best if she did it, so as not to cause a scene. She was right but he wouldn't tell Avalon that.

Begging Zara to marry him was easier than he thought it would be. He was ready to grovel for as long and hard as it took, but she agreed and now, the only thing he wanted to do was carry her back down the steps and out onto his patio where he had a pastor waiting to marry them. She was finally going to be his and he was starting to feel like the luckiest man on the planet.

The door creaked open and Avalon slipped out into the hallway. "Um," she whispered. "I think she's a little nervous. She asked to talk to you." Aiden felt his heart drop and he worried he had pushed her too much for her first day out of the hospital.

"Is she alright?" he questioned. "Has she changed her mind?" Ava didn't answer him and that made him even more nervous. Zara's best friend was usually a chatterbox and not at all afraid to speak her mind.

"Just go in and talk to her," she insisted. Aiden pushed the door open and slid past her to find Zara standing in front of the full length mirror in the dress Ava picked out for her and she took his breath away.

"You look beautiful, baby," he said. Zara didn't turn to face him, but looked at him through her reflection and her worried frown nearly sank every last hope he had of Zara becoming his today. "Ava said you were having second thoughts," he whispered.

"I can't," she sobbed. He couldn't let her finish her sentence. He crossed the room and pulled her into his arms.

"Please don't tell me you can't marry me, Zara. I feel like I've waited my whole life for you and now, this baby. The girls are so excited you are going to be their mom and when I told them about the baby, they were thrilled. Although, they both want a girl and would like to name her Princess," he said, making a face. Zara giggled through her tears and he hoped he was making some headway with her.

"I would like to veto that name, although I'm thrilled they are happy," she said. Zara carefully wiped at her eyes as if trying to avoid smearing her makeup. "And no, I'm not having second thoughts about marrying you, Aiden. It's this," she said, sobbing all over again.

Zara used her one crutch to balance herself on her good leg to carefully turn in his arms. The gown she was wearing was unzipped and from the looks of it, she was going to have trouble getting it closed. "I can't zip it up," she cried. "Ava didn't account for my expanding belly and I guess I'm not the same size now," she sniffled. He wanted to laugh but knew better than to find a hysterical pregnant woman funny.

"I don't care if you marry me in your pajamas, baby. I just want to marry you—today, right now." Aiden looked around the room and tried to come up with a plan.

"Will any of your clothes fit you, honey?" he asked. She sniffled again and nodded.

"I have jeans that will probably fit," she admitted.

"How about we make a deal," he said. Aiden slipped from his tuxedo jacket and undid his tie.

"Aiden, we can not have sex right now. I know you

think it fixes everything but it's what got us into this mess," she said, cupping her little belly.

Aiden chuckled, "No, I think we can save sex for the honeymoon portion."

"Honeymoon?" she asked.

"Yep. When you get the all clear from your doctor and can travel, I'm taking you and the girls on a little tropical getaway. Ava and Corbin are coming along too, to help watch the girls so we can have some alone time." He waggled his eyebrows at her, causing her to giggle again. "There's my girl," he praised.

"So, what's the plan then?" she asked.

"We get married in jeans and t shirts," he offered. From the look on her face, he wasn't sure she was going to agree, but then Zara's brilliant smile lit up the room and she nodded.

"I'd marry you in anything, Aiden. How about you help me change and then I'll let you carry me to the altar," she offered.

"Now, that sounds like a plan, my beautiful secret submissive," he teased.

"Hey," she grouched. "That's soon to be Mrs. Secret Submissive." Aiden wasn't sure how he had gotten so lucky finding Zara standing in that BDSM club but he wasn't going to question fate. She was his now and that was all that mattered.

Four Months Later

Aiden carried Zara over the threshold of their little bungalow. "I'm too heavy," she said. "Put me down."

"Baby, you are not too heavy," he countered. He eyed her expanding belly and she giggled.

"See, your mouth is saying all the right things but your eyes give you away, Aiden Bentley," she teased. He shut the door behind them and crossed the room to lay her on the bed. Zara looked around the room. "This is gorgeous Aiden."

He smiled down at her and wondered if wanting sex made him an ass. They had spent the better part of a day traveling to the island and he was sure his pregnant wife would be exhausted. "How about I show you what else my mouth does right," he said. Zara's eyes flared with need and he knew she was on board with his plan to get them both naked.

"Are you sure the girls will be alright with Ava and Corbin?" she asked. He loved the way she worried about his girls. They had become a family and he knew his girls loved Zara.

"I'm sure, honey. I got them a nice bungalow with plenty of space for everyone. I'm pretty sure the girls will drive Corbin half crazy and if they don't, the sight of Avalon prancing around in her bikini will finish him off."

Zara giggled and moaned, "Ugg, don't remind me about Ava and her perfect body."

He looked her up and down, "You don't have anything to worry about, baby. You're the most perfect woman on the planet," he whispered against her lips. "You're mine," he growled.

"I am," she agreed. "Forever."

"I know we've been taking it easy with your recovery, but I'd like to try something new tonight, if you're up to it," he asked. Aiden didn't want to get his hopes up but they already were.

"Yes, Aiden," she purred. "Please."

That was all the confirmation he needed. "Clothes off and get on your knees, baby," he ordered. Zara squealed and clapped, making him chuckle. "Oh, you like my command?"

"Yes," she said, breathlessly stripping out of her sundress to reveal her naked, sexy curves. He had to admit seeing Zara naked and pregnant with his baby always did crazy things to him. Lately he couldn't seem to get enough of her but he refused to push her too much. He had to squelch his dominance to just a burning ember when it came to making love to his new wife, for fear of hurting her. Now that she was medically cleared and more than willing, his inner caveman could come out to play.

Aiden ran his hands over her belly and up to cup both of her breasts. "I like these," he teased.

"Yes, well they are pretty hard to miss now that I'm pregnant. Unfortunately, my ass is twice the size it was pre-pregnancy too." She rubbed her hands over her fleshy globes, thrusting her breasts into his hands. She more than filled his palms and he couldn't wait to get his hands on her ass next.

"I think you and I see your ass very differently," he teased. "I find every sexy new curve of yours drives me completely crazy," he admitted.

"You're supposed to say that," she said. "Isn't it in the husband handbook?"

"No wife, it isn't," he said, reaching back to give her ass a playful swat. "I think I need to give that sexy mouth of yours something to keep it occupied."

She got down on her knees and smiled up at him, playfully batting her eyes. "I'm ready, Sir," she said. Aiden shucked out of his clothes, possibly setting a record for getting naked.

"Open," he ordered. He stroked his cock and loved the way her eyes seemed to follow his hand's movement up and down his staff. Zara was just as turned on by this as he was. He let her suck the tip of his cock in and nearly swallowed his own damn tongue at just how good her mouth felt. He moaned his pleasure and shoved further in, needing for her to take all of him. Aiden pulled her hair back into his hand giving him better access to watch her sucking him in and out of her mouth. He gave a little tug when she tried to take control and he set the pace, letting her know just what he wanted. He pumped in and out of her sexy mouth until he was on edge. Aiden knew if he didn't stop, he wouldn't be able to and he didn't want to finish in her mouth this time. No, he had special plans for her new curvy ass and he just hoped Zara was on board.

He pulled his cock free from her swollen lips and she mewled her protest. Aiden chuckled, "Sorry honey, but you need to catch up," he said. He helped her from her kneeling position. "Get up on the bed and spread your legs as wide as you can. I won't tie you up tonight as long as you hold still, baby. Can you do that for me?"

Zara climbed onto the bed and nodded. "Yes, Aiden. I will try." He loved her obedience, even craved it and Zara seemed to need it as much as he did. She really was the perfect woman for him. She spread her legs open, gifting him with the view of her drenched pussy. "Like this?" she questioned.

"Yes, just like that," he said, his voice hoarse with need. "Fuck, your sexy," he swore. Aiden wasted no time settling between her legs, running two fingers through her wet folds and stuffing them deep inside her. Zara cried out from the pleasure of his sudden invasion and then stilled, seeming to remember his orders. "Good girl, baby," he praised.

"Please," she whimpered. "I need to have an orgasm," she begged.

"I'm going to take good care of you, Zara," he promised. Aiden dipped his head and ran his tongue through her slick pussy, loving her taste. His girl held so still; he knew he was driving her crazy but she was being so well behaved. Aiden decided to give her exactly what she asked for. "I'm going to eat your pussy, baby and I want you to come for me," he ordered. She whimpered and nodded her head.

He lapped and sucked her sensitive folds until she couldn't seem to control her body any longer. She bucked and writhed against his mouth, taking over, finding her release. Aiden loved when she got so wild she couldn't seem to stop herself and he especially loved knowing he was the one giving her that pleasure. Zara shouted out his name as she came on his mouth and he knew it was time to tell her what he was going to do with her tonight.

Aiden kissed his way up over her belly and up the rest of the way to her mouth. He let his tongue leisurely dart into her mouth, knowing Zara would be able to taste her own release from his kiss always made him wild. "Roll over and get on your hands and knees, baby," he ordered. Zara didn't hesitate, doing exactly what he asked. He slipped from the bed to find his surprise for her he had stowed in his suitcase.

"You were such a good girl, I thought you might like another reward," he said. He pulled the purple vibrator from his bag and showed it to her. She wrinkled up her nose at it and he couldn't help his chuckle.

"A vibrator?" she questioned.

"Yes," he said. I'm going to shove this into your pussy and then I'm going to lube up that sexy ass of yours and take your virgin hole," he said. Zara gasped and moaned and he knew he was on the right track. "You like that, baby?" he asked.

"Yes," she hissed. "I've been waiting for you to take my ass, Aiden," she admitted. He had started training her ass before the accident and then he didn't want to push her, so he stopped. Now that he knew she was willing and ready, there would be no stopping him. He grabbed the lube from his bag and got back onto the bed with her, letting it dip with his weight.

"Up on your knees again and lean back against my body, baby." Zara did as ordered. "Wrap your arms back around my neck," he said. She did, laying her head to rest on his shoulder. Zara looked up at him and smiled. Aiden settled behind her and ran his hands down her body, tweaking and plucking her taut nipples. He knew she had to be ready for him but he wanted to drive her a little crazy.

"Have you ever used one of these before?" he asked. Zara studied the vibrator and shyly shook her head.

"No," she admitted. "I only used my fingers to masturbate." The thought of Zara giving herself pleasure made him nearly come up her back. He rubbed his cock against her ass and knew if he didn't get inside of her soon it would be over much too quickly.

"Um, I'd like to watch you do that sometime," he admitted. "But now, we're going to try something new."

"Okay," she said, her voice a little shaky from need or nerves. Either way, she'd forget both once he got the vibrator inside of her and turned it on. He gently guided the vibe into her pussy and she was so wet and ready for him. He turned it on and she moaned and thrust back against his body at the new sensations.

"You like that, don't you, honey?" he asked.

"Yes," she hissed.

"Good, now get on all fours again. I'm going to lube your ass and make it mine," he growled. Zara did as ordered and he squirted lube on his finger, working it into her tight opening. She was going to feel amazing. He worked his finger in and out of her ass as she rode out her first orgasm. Aiden lubed up his cock and spread her cheeks, gently nudging his way into her body. His unruly cock hated having to take his time but he wanted Zara's first experience with anal to be pleasant.

"Fuck," Zara swore, "Please Aiden, hurry. I'm going to come again," she cried. He pushed into her ass a little further and his impatient girl push back against him, taking him completely into her body. She spasmed around his dick and Aiden knew he wouldn't last long.

"Move please," she begged.

Aiden slid in and out of her ass, popping almost completely free before slamming back into her. Zara didn't protest as he dug his fingers into her hips, pumping in and out of her body. She quickly came again, shouting out his name. Aiden pulled her back against his body, loving the way she fit him. He held her so tight, he knew she was going to wear his marks in the morning.

"I'm going to come, Zara," he panted. "I can feel the vibrator inside of you." He felt every wave and pulse from the vibe he had inserted inside of Zara for her pleasure. But, it was rubbing against his cock through the thin membrane that separated her ass and her pussy and he felt about ready to explode.

"Fuck," he swore, pumping into her body twice more and then losing himself in her ass. Aiden pulled the vibrator free from her slick folds and collapsed with Zara onto the bed. "Tell me that was okay," he asked.

"That was better than okay," she said. She wrapped her arms around his neck and pulled him in for a kiss. "That was fucking fantastic," she admitted with a smile.

"Mrs. Bentley," he feigned shock. "I think your cursing has gotten worse since you married me. I must be a bad influence."

"I swear it's this pregnancy," she said, rubbing her

belly. "Either that or I'm turning into a sailor. Will you still love me if I turn into a swearing pirate?" she asked.

"Baby, I'd love you if you had a wooden leg and rocked an eye patch." Zara's laughter filled the room and Aiden was sure he'd never heard a sound more magical. He had waited his whole life to meet someone like her. She was his other half, the woman who owned his body, mind and soul—his secret submissive, and she was his.

EPILOGUE

AVALON

Avalon Michaels sat in the corner of the club and watched the couples and a few threesomes who had gathered around the room. She thought about running out of there as quickly as possible, but the thought of not facing Corbin's stupid dare head on made her feel like a coward.

She spied him as soon as he walked into the BDSM club and wasn't sure if she was worried he'd see her or if he'd find someone else more interesting and forget all about her. Corbin Eklund was a tease and she'd do well to remember that before she lost her heart to the serial player. She watched him for a few minutes and could tell the exact moment he saw her. His sexy smirk told her all she needed to know—he didn't believe she would actually take him up on his bet to show up at the club. He made his way across the crowded club and towered over her.

"I didn't think you'd show darlin'," he drawled. "What made you decide to go through with it?" Ava smiled up at him, trying not to let on what the little nickname he called her did to her. Every damn time he called her darlin', she had to bite back her moan. Frankly, everything Corbin did made her a little crazy but telling him that could never happen. He had asked her to the club because he thought she wouldn't take him up on his bet and then she'd lose at the little game they had been playing. Losing wasn't an option for her. Ava was competitive, but losing to Corbin Eklund felt worse than forfeiting to the devil himself. He was the sexiest devil she had ever met but keeping that to herself was for the best. The man already had a serious problem with humility—he had none. He was the most confident, self-possessed, arrogant man she'd ever met and for some reason, that wasn't enough for Ava to stay away from him.

"Well, a bet is a bet—so here I am. Now what are you planning on doing with me, Corbin?" she asked. Honestly, she tried not to think about the possibilities leading up to tonight. She had two very long nights to think about what she wanted him to do to her. Ava had spent the past two nights restlessly tossing and turning trying to figure out how to get through this evening with her heart intact and the answer wasn't one she easily entertained—she wouldn't.

She had met Corbin a few months prior, when her best friend, Zara hooked up with Corbin's best friend, Aiden. They stood up for their friends at their quicky wedding a few months ago when they got married. She was happy for her best friend; Zara deserved every happiness she had found with Aiden and his two little girls. But now, Ava felt more alone than ever. It wasn't as if Zara was moving away, but being the new Senator's wife was going to take up a good deal of her time. Well, that and the fact she was a new step-mother to two of the cutest little girls Ava had ever seen and Zara was pregnant with her first baby. There would be little to no time for the two of them to hang out or stay up all night talking about life and guys. Those days were over and it was time for Ava to grow up and move on.

He smiled down at her and winked. Ava rolled her eyes at just how cheesy he was but she smiled back at him. She couldn't help it—his carefree nature was infectious. She needed to relax and just enjoy tonight because it had been a damn long time since she had any fun with a man. Hell, she lost count of how many months it had been since she had sex. This night was about finding her mojo and getting back in the saddle again, nothing more. Corbin had made her no promises and she wouldn't ask for any.

"I have no idea what to do with you, Avalon," he admitted. "You showing up here caught me completely off guard."

Her smile turned quickly into a frown at his admission. She stood from her seat, "Hey if this wasn't something you wanted to happen, I can just leave. No hard feelings or anything," she sassed. Ava turned to leave and Corbin caught her by the arm.

"Stop," he commanded.

"Really Corbin, it's fine if you aren't interested," she said. Actually, it hurt like hell knowing he didn't want her but she wasn't going to stand in that damn club and cry all over him. She was stronger than that and sobbing all over a guy just wasn't her scene.

"Who the fuck says I don't want you, darlin'?" he asked. He took her hand and led it to his bulging erection, letting her feel every impressive inch of his arousal. "Does this feel like I don't want you?" Ava let her shaking fingers aimlessly run over his shaft and he groaned and leaned into her touch.

He watched her, a hungry look in his eyes and she knew he was going to give her exactly what she needed. She tried for coy, even asking, "Is that all for me?" but Corbin didn't seem to be buying her blasé question.

"Don't play with me, Ava," he whispered. "I've wanted this for too long." Hearing him admit he wanted her did strange things to her girl parts. She felt a new wetness coat her lacy panties and she was sure one touch from Corbin would set her off.

"How long, Corbin?" she almost whispered. Ava cleared her throat, "How long have you wanted me?" she questioned.

Corbin looked her up and down, as if taking in every inch of her curvy body. "I've wanted you since the first night I saw you—at Aiden's place the day the news story broke about him and Zara. You were so fucking beautiful and the way you fiercely stuck up for your friend made me hot." She had no idea Corbin even noticed her that night. She thought back to their trip to take the girls for ice cream and then the park and as far as she knew, Corbin found her annoying more than anything. Boy, had she misread the situation.

"Wow," Ava whispered.

"Yeah, wow," Corbin confirmed. "So, now that we've cleared that up, I'll ask again. What made you decide to accept my little bet and show up here?" Corbin had finally come clean with her and now it was her turn to give him some truths. She wasn't a coward but Ava knew telling him she wanted him just as much was going to sting a little. She had spent months trying to act nonchalant about anything having to do with the big guy, but seeing him now, towering over her, made Ava want to take a chance.

She went up on her tiptoes and brushed back a strand of Corbin's overly long, dark hair back from his eyes. He had the most soulful brown eyes she had ever seen. Whenever he looked at her she felt as if he could see straight into her soul. "I showed up here tonight for the same reason you did, Corbin. I want you just as much as you want me. I won't lie about that or hide behind my own insecurities."

Corbin wrapped an arm around her waist and pulled her up his body, kissing his way into her mouth. God, he tasted like bottled sunshine and she couldn't seem to get enough of him. "Thank fuck," he whispered against her lips. She wrapped her legs around his waist and he walked back to the hallway that led from the public playroom to the private rooms for exclusive members. She had only been to the club a handful of times before but Ava remembered her way around.

He opened a door and walked in, setting her on the bed that took up most of the room. "This is my private room," he said. "I thought we could do a quiet setting tonight, unless you would like to try the playroom," he offered. Ava didn't want to get into the fact she had been a guest at the club before accepting his dare tonight. Truthfully, she loved the kinky lifestyle and was training to be a sub, but telling Corbin that didn't exactly feel like "first date" material.

"This works for me," she admitted, sitting back on the bed. She didn't hide the fact she was checking Corbin out, looking his body up and down. She loved that he was dressed like a total badass tonight. Usually, he was impeccably dressed in a suit. Ava guessed that matched his whole CEO business owner day gig but tonight he was dressed to fit who he really was. Corbin filled out his black tee, showing off all his muscles and his full sleeves of tattoos. She knew he had quite a few of them hiding under his dress shirt but not full sleeves. And the way his erection pressed against his jeans almost looked painful.

"You keep looking at me like that, darlin' and this won't last very long," he growled.

"Sorry," she said. "I was just trying to figure out just how far up your tattoos go." Corbin gave her a wolfish grin and she knew she was in trouble.

"Well, I can help you figure that out, honey," he said, yanking his black t shirt up over his head. She gasped when he revealed most of his upper torso was covered in tats. She had always thought Corbin was hot, but seeing him in only his jeans, she realized he was downright beautiful.

"Corbin," she whispered. It was all Ava could manage because he literally took her breath away.

CORBIN

He watched Avalon as she looked over his upper body and when she whispered his name, all Corbin could think about was getting inside of her. He wanted her more than he wanted his next breath, but he also knew this might be his only shot with her and he needed to take his time. Tonight was a fluke, a bet he thought he was going to lose, but instead he had won the woman he was dreaming about for months now. Avalon Michaels hadn't agreed to be his, but gifting him with one night of her time was more than he could have ever hoped for.

After they all returned from Aiden and Zara's honeymoon, he convinced Ava to go out for a drink with him. At first she protested, saying she was already behind at work and making some excuse about having to get caught up with laundry. Just when he thought she was going to walk away from him, she turned back and agreed to just one drink.

He took her to his favorite little bar that had live

music loud enough they had to sit incredibly close to each other just to have a conversation. One drink turned into three and then four and before he knew it, they were both drunk and he was betting her she wouldn't go to the BDSM club where he was a member. It was the same club where Aiden met Zara, so he was hoping lightning would strike twice and somehow Ava would end up in his bed.

The next day he texted her reminding Ava about the dare she boldly accepted with the help of alcohol. He was sure her return text would tell him to go fuck himself but she didn't. Instead, she confirmed she would be at the club at nine sharp and even told him not to be late. Like he would show up even a second past nine and chance her leaving. Corbin had waited too long for something like this to fall into his lap with Ava. He wasn't about to fuck it up.

Now, they were finally in his private room and he was wondering just how much kink Avalon would allow. They really never discussed sexual likes and dislikes and this was uncharted territory for him. As a Dom, he knew communication was key and neither of them would get what they needed if he didn't ask questions. Still, he worried asking Avalon what she liked in bed was going to send her running from his room and that was the last thing he wanted.

"Hey," she said, kneeling on the bed in front of him. "Where did you just go?" she questioned. Knowing Ava knew him well enough to pick up on the fact he was worried about this next part did crazy things to his heart. She ran her hands down his face and he pulled them back up to his mouth to gently kiss her fingers and then let them rest on his chest. He liked the way she flexed them into his flesh, as if she already needed more from him, and they hadn't even gotten started yet.

"I was trying to decide how to ask you what you like—you know in bed," he said. She giggled and he took a step back from her, letting her hands fall back to her side. "That wasn't quite the response I was hoping for, Avalon," he said.

"No Corbin, I'm sorry," she said, reaching for him. "I was just laughing because I was worried about telling you what I like—you know kink wise," she admitted. He took a deep breath and a step back towards her.

"What kinds of kink do you like, Avalon?" he asked. She gasped when he ran his hands through her long dark hair, grabbing a handful of it and giving it a yank, forcing her to look up at him. She moaned and closed her eyes, telling him she liked it a little rough.

"Eyes open, darlin'," he commanded. Ava did exactly as he asked and he knew she was going to be a perfect sub. "You've done this before, haven't you honey?" he questioned. She shyly nodded her answer.

"I'm going to need more than head nods, Ava. Give me the words," he demanded. He knew he could be a little overbearing, but Avalon seemed to take everything he was throwing at her and giving him back everything in return.

"Yes, Corbin," she hissed when he tightened his grip on her hair.

"Sir," he corrected. "In here, you will call me Sir."

Avalon smiled up at him, "Yes, Sir," she corrected. "I

have done this before. I've had training to be a sub, here at the club." The thought of any other Dom taking Ava on as a sub made his inner caveman roar to life and he was pissed. There was nothing he could do about the past, but if another Dom tried to touch her, he'd break the guy in two.

"How long ago?" he questioned. He knew he was torturing himself with the details of her time at the club but he couldn't help it. Corbin needed to know before he moved forward with her.

"About a year ago. I wanted to explore this life—you know see if it was for me." He released her hair and sat down on the bed next to her. Corbin pulled Ava's small body onto his lap, loving the way she so eagerly straddled him.

"Is it?" he whispered, "the life for you?" She framed his face with her small hands again and loved the way she seemed to need to touch him.

"Yes, Sir," she whispered against his lips.

He let out his pent-up breath, not realizing he had been holding it, waiting for her answer. "I'm so fucking happy to hear you say that, Ava," he admitted.

"I take it you like it kinky then too?" she asked.

"I do," he said. "I'm a Dom and God, I've dreamed of what I want to do to you, darlin'," he said. Corbin rolled Ava under his body and pressed her into the mattress. "You're going to need a safe word, Avalon," he ordered. "I plan on taking you to the very edge of your limits and since this is our first time together, I want to be sure you are with me."

Ava smiled up at him and seemed to think for a

minute. "Ice cream," she whispered. "For the first time we met," she said.

He kissed his way into her mouth, loving the breathy little sighs and moans she gave him. He wasn't sure how he had gotten so lucky but he really didn't want to think about that right now. All Corbin wanted to do was concentrate on making Avalon his. The rest of his worries could wait until tomorrow. She hadn't made him any promises beyond the here and now and he planned on soaking up every second with her.

To be continued in Owned book 2
The End

ABOUT THE AUTHOR

Romance Rebel fighting for Happily Ever After!

K. L. Ramsey currently resides in West Virginia (Go Mountaineers!). In her spare time, she likes to read romance novels, go to WVU football games and attend book club (aka-drink wine) with girlfriends.

K. L. enjoys writing Contemporary Romance, Erotic Romance, and Sexy Ménage! She loves to write strong, capable women and bossy, hot as hell alphas, who fall ass over tea kettle for them. And of course, her stories always have a happy ending.

ABOUT THE AUTHOR

Facebook
https://www.facebook.com/kl.ramsey.58
(OR)
https://www.facebook.com/k.l.ramseyauthor/

Twitter
https://twitter.com/KLRamsey5

Instagram
https://www.instagram.com/itsprivate2/

Pinterest
https://www.pinterest.com/klramsey6234/

Goodreads
https://www.goodreads.com/author/show/17733274.K_L_Ramsey

Book Bub
https://www.bookbub.com/profile/k-l-ramsey

Amazon.com
https://www.amazon.com/K.L.-Ramsey/e/B0799P6JGJ/

Ramsey's Rebels
https://www.facebook.com/groups/ramseysrebels/

Website
https://klramsey.wixsite.com/mysite

KL Ramsey ARC Team
https://www.facebook.com/groups/klramseyarcteam/

KL Ramsey Street Team
https://www.facebook.com/groups/ramseyrebelsstreetteam/

Newsletter
https://mailchi.mp/4e73ed1b04b9/authorklramsey

ALSO BY KL RAMSEY

The Relinquished Series
Love Times Infinity
Love's Patient Journey
Love's Design
Love's Promise

Harvest Ridge Series
Worth the Wait
The Christmas Wedding
Line of Fire
Torn Devotion
Fighting for Justice

Last First Kiss Series
Theirs to Keep
Theirs to Love
Theirs to Have
Theirs to Take

Second Chance Summer Series
True North
The Wrong Mr. Right

Ties That Bind Series

Saving Valentine

Blurred Lines

Beautiful Crazy

Taken Series

Double Bossed

Double Crossed

Owned

His Secret Submissive

Coming Soon:

Alphas in Uniform

Burn For Me

Made in the USA
Columbia, SC
22 March 2023